COMING HOME

Susan Thayer Kelley

authorHOUSE®

AuthorHouse™
1663 Liberty Drive
Bloomington, IN 47403
www.authorhouse.com
Phone: 833-262-8899

This is a work of fiction. All of the characters, names, incidents, organizations, and dialogue in this novel are either the products of the author's imagination or are used fictitiously.

Published by AuthorHouse 12/14/2021

ISBN: 978-1-6655-4743-7 (sc)
ISBN: 978-1-6655-4742-0 (hc)
ISBN: 978-1-6655-4741-3 (e)

Print information available on the last page.

This book is printed on acid-free paper.

Craig Family Tree

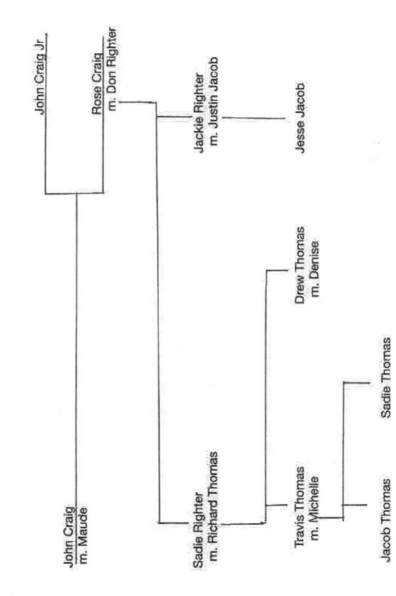

Chapter 1

She sat on the back steps of her home, or rather the Olsons' home now, for they had signed the closing papers almost a week ago. It was hard for her to believe she would be leaving her home, the home she'd lived in for the past ten years, the home she always thought she'd grow old in. It was hard for her to say goodbye to all the memories wrapped up in the home, happy memories. She allowed her mind to drift back to the day they had made the offer to buy the home, to how happy they'd been. She had been so excited to own her own home, her first home. She thought it would also be her last one, but that was not to be. The Olsons would now grow old in it instead of her. The Olsons' grandchildren would come to visit and slide down the banister, as she'd often thought her own grandchildren would do some day. The Olsons would now build the memories in her home that she would be deprived of. The thought saddened her.

She wrapped her hands around her cup of freshly made coffee and was surprised at the audible sigh that escaped from her lips. She looked up at the evening sky becoming golden as the sun began to sink low, hidden by the houses around her. There was nothing good to come of reminiscing about the past. It was time to move on.

The night was warm, too warm for sitting outside, but all the furniture was loaded onto the moving van and ready to leave, so she had made coffee and wandered outside to sit on the back steps.

Her coffee pot was the one thing she'd insisted on keeping out. No one could make a cup of coffee just like she liked. She could go out for something to eat well enough, but she needed her caffeine, and she wanted it just the way she made it, even if she had to drink it from a Styrofoam cup instead of a glass mug.

She stared up at the full moon, so beautiful and bright. *That's funny*, she thought, *how quickly the sun set and the moon showed up.* Surely it had just been seconds ago that she'd noticed the sun going down. Now here was this beautiful full moon in its place. It should be shared with someone, she knew. She took in a deep breath and exhaled slowly, wondering how she had come to this point in her life.

Again she allowed her mind to drift back to the past. She contemplated her life. Justin had married her right after she'd graduated from college. They had had a whirlwind of a romance during her last year in college, and he'd popped the question just two months before her graduation. They had decided to marry in July even though it would be hot, because he had been offered a teaching position at Texas A&M in San Antonio and had to be there ready to work when school started. Justin left in June to go to Texas, find them a place to live, set everything up, come back and get married, and move all their things down by the end of July.

She was very apprehensive about moving so far away from her family. She'd never lived anywhere else or been any farther away from them than the U of I in Illinois, and that wasn't very far. She had never even visited Texas before and didn't know anything about it other than that it was big. She wondered if she would really be able to move so far away. What if she hated Texas? And if she did, would Justin move back home, or would she be destined to live in misery?

She smiled as she recalled her apprehension back then, because she had grown to love Texas and looked upon it as her home now that she'd been there for eighteen years. She had apprehensions again about this move and hoped she would be able to look back someday and smile about the feelings she was having right now. But she was leaving, leaving Texas, her home, leaving her friends she loved, leaving her life.

Justin suddenly filled her mind, bringing the pain of the recent months to the surface. She vowed not to let the disturbing thoughts of him cloud her firm determination to leave Texas and never return. She sat staring at the back of the moving van sticking out from the side of her house in her drive.

Just then, Jesse came out of the house, interrupting her thoughts, and sat down beside her on the step. She, too, stared up at the full moon and sighed. "I guess that's it then."

"Yes, I guess it is," agreed Jackie, trying not to sound too downhearted to Jesse. "Have you got your suitcases packed?"

"Everything. What about you?"

"I just have my toiletries I plan on using tomorrow morning, but the overnight bag is ready for me to add them. I think I can get all of our suitcases and the extra boxes in the trunk and back seat. I'll put the coffee pot in the back seat along with my computer, printer, and overnight bags and pillows.

"I hope you kept a sweater out in case it gets chilly at night," she added as an afterthought.

"I did. And I also packed two pairs of pajamas in my overnight bag, one long-sleeved pair and one sleeveless. I have no idea what the weather will be like up there, so I figured I'd better have both just in case."

"I'm sorry I wasn't much help to you," Jackie lamented. "There was just so much to think about, so much to do, so you were pretty much on your own, but you've done quite well, not only in taking care of your own things but in helping me as well. I'm proud of you, Jess."

"I wanted to be as much help as possible. I knew you had a lot on your mind. If I didn't get something right, I guess we'll find out later."

Jackie smiled at Jesse. It seemed Jesse had grown up a lot in the past couple of months. Lord knew she had no choice but to. It just wasn't right. A child should be able to relax during their short time as a young one, enjoy life, not worry about anything other than grades, friends, and boyfriends. Jackie realized her daughter was now going to become like so many other children—hurt, lost, trying to find their way in such a harsh, unloving world. If there was just some way to shield kids from all the hurt. But too many times, life dealt the hand, and the adults had no choice but to play it as best as they saw fit, which wasn't always in the best interest of the children. At least she vowed to try very hard to never hurt Jesse the way Justin had. She would be her protector.

They were quiet for a few minutes before Jesse said, "Mom, what's going to happen to us?"

Jackie was as apprehensive about the future as her daughter was, but she was trying to be positive about this move. "We'll be all right, I promise."

"Are you sure we couldn't have stayed here, at home?" Jesse asked.

"I wish we could. But you know I couldn't afford to keep the house without your father's income. It's just too expensive."

"But I don't understand why we couldn't have waited till this time next year to move. Even if we couldn't stay in this house, we could get an apartment or rent something else till the school year next year is over. I really want to finish high school here where all my friends are, with only one more year to go. I won't know anyone in a new school."

"Jesse," Jackie said, "we've been through this. I know you want to stay here. I've thought and thought about what is best for us, and right now, I think it would be best for both of us if we had family close by. They will be a tremendous help to us; family always is when there's trouble. And I really think it's best that we go now, before you finish school, expressly so you can have a year of school to make some friends. If we should wait to move a year from now, how will you be able to make friends your age after you've graduated? This way, you can take your time during the school year and make some friends, and come next summer, you'll have your group established, and you'll really enjoy the summer before college. I'm certain of it."

"I guess you're right," relented Jesse. "I just hate to leave the ones I've grown up with. I'll probably never see any of them anymore, ever."

Jackie sat her coffee cup down and drew her daughter close to her, pulling her head down onto her shoulder and stroking her hair. "I know, honey. I know. If I could, I would make all of this go away. If I could, I'd give you that great big moon up there so it could shine down on you always, no matter where you are, and make your life happy. If I could, you know I would."

"I know, Mom. I love you so much. You're the best mom in the whole world."

Jackie chuckled. "I doubt that, and I hope you always feel that way. We're going to get through this, and we'll be the better for it. Let's just promise to stay close and be there for each other. You know I'll need your strength to help me just as much as you'll need mine."

"I promise. But what about when I go off to college? Who will be there for you then?"

"That is another reason I want to leave now. If we're settled and making friends in a new place this summer, by next year when you leave, I should be well established and settled in a new job with some new friends. This really is the best thing for us to do. I'm fully convinced of that."

"But," Jesse said, "why do we have to go all the way back to Illinois? Why couldn't we just stay here in Texas?"

"I guess because it just seemed like the place I needed to be, close to my family right now. And I'd like you to become close to them too."

Jesse pulled away from her mother and went to check the back of the trailer loaded with all their possessions. When she returned, she said, "They locked it all up. It's ready to go. I guess there's nothing left to do but say goodbye to our house and go."

"I guess you're right," agreed Jackie. However, neither of them made a move. Instead, Jesse sat back down on the step.

"Mom, why did Dad do it?"

Jackie was startled by the question, one she had asked herself many times in the past couple of months. "I wish I knew, baby," she answered.

"Doesn't he love us anymore?"

"You know he loves you, honey. He's just confused right now." She wished that could be the truth, but in reality, she knew Justin wasn't confused. He had fallen out of love with her somewhere along the way. However, Jackie wanted to steer away from that conversation. The pain was too great right now to confront. Eventually, though, she would have to address some things with Jesse to try to help her understand why things sometimes turned out the way they did, even if she didn't fully understand it herself.

"Mom?" said Jesse.

"Yes?"

"I'm scared."

"Me too, honey. Me too. But let's not think about that right now. For now, let's just get through tonight, find a room, and tomorrow we'll be on our way."

Chapter 2

They found a room for the night in a local motel and began their long trek to Illinois the next morning. By the middle of the afternoon, Jesse had grabbed a pillow and tried to get some sleep. Jackie looked over at her slumbering daughter and smiled. Jesse had been stoic upon leaving their home the night before, refusing to cry, even though Jackie knew she was very near to it. Justin had come by to say goodbye to Jesse and her, but she'd refused to speak to him, other than to tell him that if he needed to reach Jesse, he could phone her mother.

Jackie had gone into the house to pack her last-minute things, unplug the coffee pot and wash it up, and set everything by the front door. She'd taken her time so Justin and Jesse could have some private time for their goodbyes. She heard Jesse and Justin talking on the front porch and was certain she heard Jesse sobbing. Jackie hoped Justin felt like the dog he was for what he'd done to his little girl. She hoped Jesse had caused him to regret his selfishness.

Jackie allowed her mind to drift while she drove. She thought of how she'd learned she was pregnant within three months of their wedding. She hadn't wanted a child so soon after marrying but was certain it had been her fault. She had been so involved with moving, and everything was so new, she'd forgotten to take her birth control pill one night. Jesse was the result. Now she was very happy at having made the mistake. What would she have done without her Jesse, especially now?

She thought about a conversation she and Justin had had about what to name the baby. If it was a boy, they'd agreed on Joshua, and Jesse if it was a girl. She had laughed when Justin suggested they name the baby with a name that began with J because both of their first names began with J, as well as their last name. At first, Jackie thought he was joking, but the more she thought about it, the more she liked the idea. Now the only regret she had was that Jesse's middle name was Justine, after Justin. Why hadn't she insisted on naming her after herself?

She remembered her labor when Jesse was born. Justin had been there holding her hand, coaching her breathing, just as they'd been taught. He was so supportive of her then. The perfect husband. And he'd been the perfect father throughout Jesse's growing up. He'd taught her to read before she even began school, and he had always been there for her whenever she scraped her knees playing, or when she was afraid of the dark, or when she needed to be tickled. He'd been there for her piano recitals, baseball games, and later cheerleading practices. He'd been so caring of her, of Jesse. Jackie had assumed it would go on forever, that she and Justin would grow old together and play with their grandchildren after Jesse got married.

Then it struck her that Justin might not walk Jesse down the aisle. Would he? Would Jesse even want him to? Yes, she decided, Justin would if Jesse wanted him to. Jackie would see to it, come hell or high water, even if Jackie would prefer that he not be informed of the wedding at all. She became so angry with Justin that she raised her hand, made a fist, and was ready to pound it onto the steering wheel, but caught herself just in time as she looked over at Jesse sleeping beside her. Instead, she shook her fist at the air while gritting her teeth in anger.

She chastised herself for feeling so hateful toward Justin. Hate, she knew, could eat away at the inside of a person until they became bitter and vengeful. She would never allow that to happen to her. She vowed that from then on, she would be civil to Justin, no matter how it killed her inside. She would do it for Jesse. She would not let this destroy her. She would be a positive person. She would win!

Her mind began to turn to her mother. She knew her mother would have questions. This worried her. How would she handle the questions? What would she say? What could she say? How could she answer how this had happened when she didn't know herself? Had she done anything to bring this on? She didn't know. How could she handle questions when she wasn't ready to talk about any of it, to anyone?

She had lain awake night after night, going over the events that had happened in her life the past two months. She would eventually fall asleep and awake to puffy red eyes from the tears she had been unable to stop. She had tortured her soul to try to make sense of it, yet no answers had come. She seemed even more bewildered than ever because there just was no reason in her mind for Justin's actions.

Jesse began to stir beside her, slowly waking, stretching, and yawning. "Where are we?" she inquired.

"Little Rock isn't too far down the road. We should be there in about a half hour. Did you have a nice nap?"

"If you call it nice to be slouched sideways while you have this strap across your neck," she answered as she pulled on the seat belt.

"I know. It really is impossible to get comfortable with that around you, isn't it? But at least you're safe with it on. With all these big trucks on the road, I certainly wouldn't take it off.

"Would you like to stop in Little Rock and get a bite to eat? Maybe stretch our legs a bit?"

"Definitely!" Jesse said. "How far will we get tonight?"

"Oh, I don't know. I thought we'd just drive until we decide we've had enough for one day and then find a room for the night. Of course, you know the farther we go today, the less we'll have to go tomorrow." Jackie gave her a daughter a glance to see her reaction to that.

"And why would I be in a hurry to get there tomorrow? To what?"

"I know, Jesse. I understand how you feel, really I do. I just thought perhaps you'd rather be in the car for one long day instead of two. I'll tell you what. We'll stop when you're ready. You make the decision."

That was agreed upon, and then Jesse said, "Tell me about Illinois. What's it like in the summer?"

"It's lush and green. It's really quite beautiful. The trees are so varied, some extremely tall and others short and flowering. And the corn is really tall too. They used to say, 'Knee high by the Fourth of July,' but that was way back. Now with modern technology, they can get the crops planted in about half the time, so they have a longer growing season. So now the corn is at least as tall as an elephant's eye by Fourth of July."

Jesse laughed. "You just made that up."

"No, really, I've heard that saying, too, somewhere, but I don't know where. Anyway, getting back to Illinois in summer, it can be quite hot because the humidity is usually high, partly because of the corn. I remember before my parents had air-conditioning, we'd bring a blanket outside, where we kids would lay looking up at the stars through Dad's binoculars he got in the navy, while Mom and Dad would visit with the neighbors doing the same thing. It was the only way to get cool. Anyway, I think you'll like it."

"Why didn't we ever go to visit Grandma and Grandpa in the summer? We always went in winter."

"Mostly because we were sick and tired of the heat in Texas and wanted to get away to some cold climate occasionally, some snow and ice. Do you remember sledding down the hills behind Grandma and Grandpa Craig's house?"

"And then we'd come inside, half-frozen, to drink her hot chocolate she'd have ready for us," Jesse added.

"She always made the best hot chocolate, didn't she? And she made it from scratch. None of this instant stuff like we buy. And she'd top it off with those big marshmallows. And you would always eat your marshmallows and then ask for more before ever tasting the chocolate."

"Well, I had to let the chocolate cool before I could drink it."

"So you always said. I always thought that was just an excuse to get more marshmallows."

"It worked, didn't it?" They both laughed.

Jackie said, "And I think we always came back in winter because you were out of school for the holidays. Justin was off work, too, so all in all, it just seemed like the right time to go."

Jesse said, "Why did it always feel like we were going back in time when we'd go to Grandma and Grandpa's house?"

"Which grandma and grandpa are you talking about, the Craigs or the Righters?"

Jackie thought Jesse was speaking about her great-grandparents.

"Well, I did feel that way at the Craigs' too, but I knew that was because they lived on a farm. But I wasn't talking about either of my great-grandparents. I meant your mom and dad's house."

"Oh." Jackie thought a minute. "Maybe because of their house and because they live in such a small town that really does seem to be stuck in time. The storefronts go back to the turn of the twentieth century, and they even have the old brick streets in part of the town. They try to keep the town that way. It's what draws the tourists in the summer. Then there's the Amish who would come to town in their horse and buggies."

"Oh, yes, I forgot about them. They're still there, I suppose."

"Yes, I'm sure they are. I'm so sorry, Jesse, that we lived so far from your grandparents' home and we didn't go back nearly often enough for you. I guess we got so wrapped up in living our lives that we neglected going for visits as often as we did when you were smaller."

"Well, it wasn't like I had the time either with all the things I've been involved with in school. I guess I'll get a taste of your childhood now though, won't I?"

"I'm afraid things won't really be like they were when I grew up there. Times have changed everything. And I was trying to remember the last time we came up for a visit. It seems like it was right after Justin got a raise, so that's why we decided to fly instead of drive. I just don't remember when it was."

"I was in fifth grade. I remember because while I was in Illinois, I met James Talbot there, and I thought I was in love. I was sure I was going to die when we had to go back home. Do you remember him?"

"The scrawny little boy down a block from Mom and Dad? Jim and Martha Talbot's boy?"

"He wasn't scrawny! He was … lanky. And he had big, beautiful brown eyes, and he was in seventh grade. I thought he was so much older than I was." She chuckled upon remembering, then added, "And all the time I was google eyeing him, he never even knew I existed."

"Well, I suppose that's the way it is when you're all of, what, eleven maybe?" Jackie laughed.

Jesse went on, "I wonder whatever became of him."

"Maybe you could go down the block and ask his parents," Jackie chided.

"Not on your life!" Jesse was appalled at the thought.

"Well, I can tell you one thing," Jackie said. "If he is still around town today, I'm certain he wouldn't be able to ignore you anymore."

"Oh, Mom, stop," Jesse protested. "He's probably off to college somewhere by now anyway."

"Maybe so, but he might come home for the summer. You never know. You might just run into him." Jackie peeked at her daughter out of the corner of her eye.

Jesse seemed deep in thought at the possibility before continuing, "I wonder if he's still as good-looking as he used to be. He's probably grown up ugly and pimply faced." They both had a good laugh at that thought.

"You know," Jackie continued, "every summer they have a huge festival in town, and hundreds, if not thousands, come from miles around for it. I know they still have it because Mom mentioned it last summer after it was over. She entered a pie in the pie contest and won first place. She is the best pie maker around, you know. Anyway, about the festival, I used to look forward to it so much—lots of junk food to eat and bands and dancing. Now there's a place to meet people. I wonder when it will be this year.

"Well, here is the outskirts of Little Rock, so start looking for a place to stop and eat."

They ended up at a Cracker Barrel, then walked around a little before climbing back into the car. Soon they were headed east again on I-40, this time with Jesse behind the wheel.

Chapter 3

They arrived at Jackie's parents' home by the middle of the next afternoon. Her parents came out to greet them. Rose, her mother, embraced them, and then her father, Don, did. Don started to open the trunk to get the suitcases out, but Jackie stopped him, telling him they could do that later. What she really wanted first was to unwind, find out how everyone was, and catch up on a little gossip.

Rose walked Jackie toward the house, arm in arm, leaving Don to escort Jesse inside. "Well, Sadie and Richard are coming over tomorrow for dinner and bringing their kids. She wanted to come today, but I told her you'd need some time to get settled in and you'd probably be tired today."

"You've got that right," Jackie agreed. Jackie stopped to look at the house. "I forgot just how magnificent this old house is. We were talking on the way up and decided it's been six and a half years since our last visit."

"Much too long, I might add," her mother said. Then squeezing her daughter's arm tighter, she added, "Oh, it's so good to have you here. You have no idea how good it is. I'm just so happy."

"I know, Mom." Then she turned to her father and said, "It looks like you're keeping the place up well, Dad."

"Yes, but it's getting harder and harder on your old dad. I keep telling Rose it's time to downsize, but she says, 'Maybe next year,' every time I bring it up. I think she's trying to kill me off so she can collect on my insurance policy."

They all laughed before Rose said, "Come on. I want to show you something."

She led them inside, where Jackie came to an abrupt stop. Taking a deep breath, she asked, "Is that apple pie I smell?"

Rose was beaming. "It certainly is. Come on. I'll put a pot of coffee on, and we'll cut it." The aroma of apple pie was what Rose had wanted to show Jackie. She had remembered that it was Jackie's favorite and had made it especially for her. Jackie felt warm inside to know her mother would do something special just for her. It was her way of saying, "I love you."

They sat around the kitchen table chatting about the trip from Texas, about what Rose was doing to keep busy these days, and how Don's work was. He was sixty-four and thinking of retiring soon, he told her. He'd been entertaining offers on the machine shop he'd owned since before Jackie was born. "What will you do if you retire? You're too young to just sit around."

"Like I said outside, this house takes a good deal to keep it up, and Rose is always wanting something or other done to it. She'll have to take you out back to see her latest project. And if I run out of things to do, I could always get a part-time job welcoming customers at the Walmart store." He chuckled.

Jackie looked shocked. "You've got to be kidding! You have a Walmart store here now?"

Don answered, "Yes, and it's going to be the ruination of our little town."

Rose reprimanded him with "Now, Don, don't get started on that again." Turning to Jackie, she said, "He's upset because our hardware store just went out of business, and he can't go down and buy just one or two screws anymore. Now he has to buy ten and throw eight away."

"That's exactly right," agreed Don, fuming.

"Mom, how is Sadie and her crew doing? We don't keep in touch the way we should. Is she still working at the telephone office?"

Sadie was Jackie's older sister by three years, and they'd grown up close to each other. Sadie had married a local boy she'd gone to school with, and he'd done well for himself and his family as an editor of their local newspaper. They had stayed in the area instead of moving away as

Jackie had. Jackie had always been glad of that, because she'd wanted someone close to watch over her parents.

Rose answered, "That office would close if it weren't for Sadie. I don't know why she works so hard though. Richard makes enough money."

"But, Mom, there are more reasons for working than to make money, you know," Jackie countered.

"So you say. In my book, that's the only reason for a woman to work. Women have enough to do at home." She looked like she was about to say something else but thought better of it. "Jesse," she said instead, "do you want to go check out the rest of the house?"

Jesse said she'd love to see it again. After she left the room, Rose said to Jackie, "So how's she taking things, Jackie? Do you think she'll be all right?"

Jackie bristled at the question. "She'll be fine, Mother. Jesse and I have a good relationship, and I think she'd let me know if she's having trouble."

"But this is all so sudden. It just isn't something I ever expected of Justin."

Jackie rose from the table. "I think it's time we brought our suitcases in from the car, Dad. Would you help me?"

"Sure, honey," he replied after gulping the last of his coffee down.

When they were outside, Don said, "Don't give your mother any heed. She's just worried about you. That's all."

"I know, Dad. It's all right. I knew she'd have questions. I just wish I had the answers."

"Don't hurry it, sweetie. Don't do anything yet. Just wait and see. That's the best advice I can give you. And you know your mother and I are here if you want to talk."

"I know. Thanks, Dad." Jackie gave him a peck on the cheek.

Jesse came out to help bring things in, chatting aimlessly about how massive the house was, how she'd forgotten how big it really was, and about the changes she noticed from the last time they visited. Don and Rose had picked up the old Victorian mansion for a steal before Jackie was born and had poured their hearts and souls into it to bring it back to the grandeur it had in its early years. Rose had fallen in love with it immediately and had wanted it so badly Don just couldn't tell her no, even though he could see how much work it would take. He had grown to love the home as much as Rose did over the years. Now neither one could conceive of living anywhere else, even if it was getting to be almost too much for them to take care of.

Rose was in the kitchen getting supper started when Jackie entered after unpacking. "Jesse's quite excited to be able to stay here, you know," she said to her mom. "She settled into the room with the wallpaper with the roses. By the way, I really like the new look in that room. The dark taupe with the red roses seems to fit the time period of the house."

"Thank you. Actually, Sadie found that paper for me at an outlet wallpaper store, and I just couldn't resist. Don wasn't too happy at having to hire someone to hang it. He wanted to try it himself, and I put my foot down. Can you imagine your father wrestling with wallpaper?" They both chuckled at the thought.

Jackie helped her mother in the kitchen for a while before Rose turned to her and said, "Jackie, I'm sorry if I upset you earlier. I didn't mean to."

Jackie replied, "It's all right. I'm not upset. I guess this is all so recent, and I just need more time to sort things out."

"Honey, may I give you a piece of advice?"

"Sure."

"Just don't be too hasty in wanting a divorce. Give it a little time first. You never know. Justin might come to his senses, and you two might get back together."

Jackie chuckled. "Funny. Dad told me the exact same thing a while ago. I won't do anything rash. I promise. I'm just not sure, though, that we ever could get back together. I mean, he's broken the trust I had in him, and I'm not sure I could ever get it back."

"I know you feel that way now, but that too might change, given time." Rose bit her lip in contemplation of where to go from here. She decided to drop it for now and turned back to her stove.

Jackie, however, needed someone to talk to. She decided maybe she did need to talk about it with her mother. "But," she continued, "how do I compete with the younger women? How would I ever be able to keep my husband's interest in me, and me alone, with all those good-looking babes out there just waiting to get Justin in bed with them?"

"I don't think you need to feel like you're competing with them. Justin knows you; he knows your good points and your flaws. You two have been married for what, eighteen, nineteen years? He might believe right now that what he wants is someone younger, but given time, he might come to his senses and realize what he lost was much more than youth and good looks."

"But how could I be certain it won't happen again?"

Rose turned to her daughter. "How did you know when you married him that it wouldn't happen the first time? There's always that risk. And when someone is as good-looking as Justin, it increases the risk. You took that risk when you married him, and you might just have to take that risk again, if you two should get back together."

Jackie thought about that. Her mother was right, she knew. If a person lived on what-ifs, they'd never do anything for fear of *what if.* That was something she had never considered before, that she had taken a risk in marrying Justin in the first place. She had always known they were truly in love, and because she knew she would not even consider looking at another man, she had assumed Justin would always be the same way.

"I don't think …" Jackie paused before continuing. She didn't want to begin to cry and was getting close to it. She composed herself before saying, "I don't think it would have hurt so much if he'd come to me and talked about his feelings. We could have maybe worked it out. But instead, he just came home one day and said he was packing a bag and leaving me." She snapped her fingers. "Just like that, he packed and was gone. No discussion! No nothing! I was totally bewildered."

"And you probably wondered what you did wrong. What did you do to make him fall out of love with you?"

"Yes!" Jackie couldn't believe her mother understood so well just what Jackie had been torturing herself with. "And then he never phoned, never called Jesse. That really hurt." Then the tears did well up, and she blinked trying to get them to go away. When they wouldn't, she crossed to the paper towel holder and blotted her eyes.

Rose came over, put her arms around her daughter, and tried to comfort her. "I'm so sorry, Jackie. I wish there was some way I could make it all go away. And there is always a lot of hurt and finger pointing at each other at times like this."

"How can I point a finger at someone if he doesn't even make an attempt to talk things out? If he doesn't let me know he's disappointed in our marriage, how can I know what I should change, how to improve? As it is, I don't know if there was anything I could have done differently. He didn't even give me that chance."

"Maybe he couldn't talk to you about it right then. That's why you need to give it some time. Maybe later, he'll feel like talking."

"Well, right now, the way I feel, it's too late for talking."

"You're hurt too much right now."

"You're certainly right about that!"

Jesse came into the kitchen then to see what was for supper, so Jackie and Rose ended their conversation and busied themselves with preparations. Jesse ended up with the job of setting the dining room table.

They had a pleasant meal and afterward spent the evening on the front porch, sipping lemonade. Jesse excused herself so she could use the shower before her mom needed it, since they would be sharing a bathroom. There were two baths on the second floor, one for three bedrooms to share, and one for the master bath, which originally had been a bedroom split down the middle and turned into two baths. There was a half bath on the main floor, tucked up under the stairway in the entry hall. Because the age of the home dated to the late 1800s, it had been built before indoor bathrooms, and someone before Don and Rose had added them, although Don had redone each one after purchasing the home.

Afterward, Jesse intended to begin reading the new book by John Grisham she'd picked up a couple of weeks before moving. She figured she would have plenty of time to read it once they moved, since she didn't know anyone in Illinois and would be looking for things to do to keep herself busy.

After Jesse dismissed herself, Rose said, "I think you're right, Jackie. Jesse seems like she'll be just fine. Maybe tomorrow I can get her to run a couple of errands for me and then help me with dinner for tomorrow night. If we keep her busy, she'll adjust to her new surroundings better."

"Thanks, Mom." Jackie couldn't agree more.

Don said, "But what about you, Jackie? What do you intend to do to keep busy?"

"Well," she began, "I figured the first thing I should do is look for a job and then a place to live."

"Now, Jackie," began Don, "there's no reason to find another place to live. Rose and I have way too much house here for us, and we'd love to have you two stay here. Actually, we both could use a little help around here. You see, my intentions are purely selfish. The truth of the matter is Rose needs help keeping her part of the house up, the cleaning and things like that."

"Oh, Don, stop!" cried Rose. "I can do my part! You're the one who probably needs help. But I wouldn't want Jackie to feel like she has to come here to take care of two old geezers. But I would love to have you stay with us, Jackie. You know you're always welcome at home."

"I know," Jackie said. "But Jesse's always had space to have her friends in whenever she wants, and, well, quite frankly, sometimes they can play their music a little too loudly for you two *old geezers*." She poked at her dad's arm with a twinkle in her eye.

Don said, "No need to decide tonight. Let's just take it one day at a time and see how things go. You never know. I might even get up and shake a leg with the young kids."

"That I'd like to see." Rose chuckled.

Don commented that the night felt warm for early June, and Rose wondered if it was a sign that they were in for a hot summer. Jackie thought it felt great because when they left Texas, it was already in the nineties during the days and high seventies at night. She even thought it felt a little brisk for her but decided it was because she wasn't used to the climate change yet. She laid her head back on the porch swing, closed her eyes, and tried not to think. It was hard not to think when she didn't want to, but it was too painful to think. She just wanted to forget. She would have liked a stiff drink but knew her mother and father had nothing stronger than coffee in their house.

Chapter 4

Rose seemed to keep Jesse busy all the next day with first one thing and then another, for which Jackie was eternally grateful.

Sadie, Richard, and their two boys, Travis and Drew, and their wives and kids came over. Actually, Travis was the only one with two kids, while Drew's wife had one still in the oven, as they'd often joked. Travis had a boy and a girl, ages two years and six months respectively.

Jackie couldn't get over how everyone and everything had changed, except her sister, who seemed the same. The biggest changes were in the kids. She still thought of Travis and Drew as kids. She was feeling older by the minute. The last time she saw them, Travis was almost Jesse's age now, seventeen, and Drew had been fifteen. It was hard to imagine them grown-up with families of their own.

Jackie even commented to Sadie that everyone must be getting married quite young these days. Sadie agreed but said it was because in small towns, there wasn't much else to do. Then Sadie added, "I know you waited till you were finished with college to get married, but if you remember right, I had Travis when I was twenty, and I had already been married for two years."

"I guess you're right. I did get married at an old age, didn't I? I was all of twenty-one and had Jesse before I turned twenty-two." They both laughed. Jackie let out a sigh and lamented, "What I wouldn't give to be back then at that age."

"Me, too, but leave the stupidity out that seems to go with being young." This brought another round of laughter.

The women got busy in the kitchen, while the men gathered in the den. Jesse was in the backyard with the little ones. The family was truly happy to be together again, and they spent the afternoon getting reacquainted. Jesse especially enjoyed the two little ones. She fed and put the baby down for a nap shortly before dinner so everyone could eat without interruptions, then agreed to take Travis's son, Jacob, out to swing in the backyard again after dinner and before his nap.

The men retreated to the den right after dinner to watch a football game on TV, while the four women cleaned up after dinner. It was so good to have the family all together again, Rose contemplated. She was truly happy, and it showed.

Jackie watched her mother while she worked and hoped she could one day be as well-adjusted in her old age as her mother obviously was. Jackie was envious, though, of Sadie and her son's families. They were still all together, with mates, as it should be. She felt as if she didn't fit in with the family. A part of her was missing, and it saddened her. No one had gotten a divorce in the Righter family, Jackie's maiden name, or on the Craig side, Rose's maiden name, as far as she knew. Would she be the first? If it led to that, she would probably loathe family gatherings in the future. She feared the family would snicker about her behind her back as the black sheep of the family, the one who couldn't keep her man from wandering. Did they already feel that way about her?

While they were working in the kitchen, Sadie said, "Oh, Jackie, it's so good to have you back here after so many years. We have so much catching up to do. I can take you around to all the neat novelty shops that have opened here in the last several years, and there's a fairly new tearoom just east of downtown in one of the Queen Anne homes on Main Street that you've just got to go to. We'll have so much fun."

Jackie looked at her. "Now, Sadie, I'm not here on vacation, you know. I'm going to have to work and watch every penny I make. I doubt I'll have the time or the funds to go running around all over the countryside with you. At least not for quite a while."

Sadie looked hurt but said she understood. Jackie felt bad about what she'd said, so she added, "But maybe I could go with you to some shops on a Saturday as long as I only look."

"That would be great." Sadie brightened up. "Why don't we plan on next Saturday?" They agreed on it and finished up the kitchen.

Rose went into the den with Michelle and Denise, Travis's and Drew's wives, while Sadie and Jackie sat at the kitchen table with a second cup of coffee in hand. Jackie wanted desperately to talk to Sadie, to unload on her, but knew it would not be a good time with all the family around. Jackie had always confided in Sadie, relying on her more mature wisdom and experience. The fact that Jackie had always looked up to her older sister in that way was what had drawn them close together and kept them close throughout the teenage years. Even after Jackie moved away, they kept in touch, mostly by phone, keeping up on what the other was doing. It hadn't been until the past two or three years that they allowed time to lapse without speaking regularly. And often when they did, it was about Don or Rose as the underlying cause for the call. Jackie wondered how they had allowed that to happen to them.

Jackie said, "I'm looking forward to next Saturday. Do you know how long it's been since just the two of us did something together, alone?"

"Won't you be bringing Jesse with you?" asked Sadie.

"I don't think I want to. I really feel like I need to talk with you, so I thought it could be just the two of us."

Sadie put her coffee cup down, reached across the table, and covered Jackie's hand with her own. "Oh, Jackie, I feel just terrible for you, and for Jesse too. Listen, if you want to talk, why don't you come over to my house tomorrow night, and we can talk then?

That way, Jesse can come with you next Saturday. I know she'd love to go with us, and I think you need to talk to me before Saturday."

Jackie agreed just as Jesse opened the back door and brought Jacob, Travis, and Michelle's two-year-old son back inside. Jesse was bubbling over with information about this awesome little two-year-old who spoke like an adult. She was bowled over at how smart he seemed. And she confided that someday she wanted one just like him, which brought a smile to Sadie's and Jackie's faces.

Michelle and Denise entered the room then, and each took a seat at the table. Michelle said, "The room in there sure is boring. Football, ugh!"

Jackie asked Denise how her pregnancy was going. Was she having a girl or a boy? What name had they picked?

Denise stated that the last sonogram indicated a girl, but she wasn't entirely convinced. She had heard that sometimes sonograms were wrong when it seemed to be a girl, that quite possibly something was hidden. She wasn't counting on anything just yet. She still had the better part of three months to go and had plenty of time to get the nursery ready. The name picking was still in the discussion stage. She asked if there were any suggestions anyone would like to entertain.

They all thought a minute before Sadie offered a couple of names that were quickly rejected. Then Jackie said, "By the way, Michelle, how did you and Travis decide to name your son Jacob? That couldn't possibly be after us, could it?"

"As a matter of fact, it is. Jacob is a good first name, even if it is your last name.

And you just happen to be Travis's favorite aunt. He often spoke of how you would take him and Drew back into the woods on treks whenever visiting your grandpa Craig's house. He says you were always ready to play with the kids. It was his idea to name Jacob after your last name."

Jackie smiled. "I had no idea. That is truly wonderful. I feel so privileged. And in that case, why don't you name yours after us also, Denise? We have more names than our last name to use."

That brought a round of laughter from everyone. Rose entered the kitchen then and said, "It sounds like you're having a lot more fun in here than what's going on in there."

"We were just giving Denise ideas about what to name the baby," offered Sadie. "And Jackie just found out Michelle's little Jacob is named after them, so she offered to let Denise name her baby after them as well."

"What a splendid idea," agreed Rose. "If it's a girl, you could name her Maude."

"Maude!" A cry went up from most of the women in the room, except Sadie and Rose, who were laughing hysterically.

Jackie looked horrified. "Mom!" she protested. "Really! I can't believe you'd say such a thing, let alone think it."

"Who's Maude?" asked Jesse. "We don't have anyone in our family named Maude."

"Oh, yes you do," answered Rose.

"Mother, please," Jackie protested further. "Why don't we just change the subject. I'm sorry I brought the whole thing up."

"Haven't you told Jesse?" Rose asked. "I can't believe it."

Jesse said, "Told me what? What about Maude? Tell me."

Rose answered, "Your mother's real name is Maude. You didn't know, huh?

Well, I'm not surprised. She always hated her name."

Jesse's eyes widened. She turned to Jackie and asked, "Mom, is that true? Your name is Maude?"

Jackie said, "All right. Now that it's out, you might as well know the truth. Yes, my name is really Maude. I hated the name and chose the name Jackie when I was eight years old, and I've been going by Jackie ever since. There. Are you happy now?" she said, looking at her mother.

Rose said, "You see, Jesse, she was named after my mother, your great-grandma Craig. Her first name is also Maude."

Jesse still looked shocked and just stared at her mother. Jackie continued, "Well, wouldn't you hate the name Maude if it were your name? Just say the name three times and really listen when you do at how it sounds. And Mom used to call me Maudie when I was little, which was worse."

Jesse said, "Well, how did you come upon the name Jackie to go by then?"

Rose answered for Jackie, "When your mom was little, she used to run. She was always running around the yard playing, never walking. Always running. Someone in the family called her a jackrabbit one day, and after that, people would say, 'Where's our little jackrabbit?' Since everyone began calling her that, she decided that Jackie was better than either Maude, Maudie, or Jackrabbit. So, one day she marched in and declared she was no longer Maude but Jackie. After that, if anyone called her Maude, she would stubbornly refuse to answer them or even acknowledge anyone was speaking to her."

"And I'd just as soon we leave it that way, if you please," Jackie said. "I really thought I'd left that name in the dust long ago. I'd just as soon leave it dead and buried."

"You know," Rose continued, "your grandma Craig wasn't too happy about you dropping her name. She was always so proud that you were named after her."

"Well, I'm still named after her. It says so on my birth certificate."

"Yes, I suppose so. All the same, she liked having another Maude running around, I think. But I told her years ago not to take it so personally, that it had nothing to do with her. She's gotten over it.

"By the way, speaking of Grandma Craig, she will want to see you two as soon as possible. Do you think you could find time to go visit them sometime soon?"

Jackie looked at Jesse, who gave a shoulder shrug. "Sure, we could go maybe Tuesday. What do you say, Jesse?"

"That's fine."

"Actually," Rose went on, "Mom could use some help doing some things around their house. You know they are getting up there in years now, mid-eighties, and really needing a helping hand now and then. Dad mentioned his windows could use a washing outside, if you wouldn't mind."

Jackie groaned but agreed to do them when they went on Tuesday. She figured this was payback for being gone for years and getting out of that kind of help in the past.

Monday evening after dinner, Jackie excused herself from Jesse and her parents to go to Sadie's house. Jesse had taken Rose to the video store earlier and rented a thriller Jesse was certain her grandparents would enjoy. She stated firmly to Jackie that she'd be fine with her grandparents, a good movie, and a bowl of popcorn for the evening. She told her mother to go out and have a good time and not to think about her.

Sadie was waiting for Jackie when she arrived. Richard had found an excuse to leave the house so the two could be alone. Jackie smelled the coffee immediately upon entering the front door.

After they had their coffee cups in hand and were seated at the kitchen table, Sadie began, "So tell me about everything that's happened."

"Sadie, that's just it. Nothing really happened. That's why I just don't understand this. There were no fights, not even disagreements. He just came home one day, stated he had fallen in love with someone else, packed his bags, and left. I tried to get him to wait and talk with me about it, but he said there wasn't anything to talk about. He had thought it over and decided he wanted the other woman."

"And you don't know any more than that?"

"Absolutely nothing! I don't know her age, her name, how they met, or where he went when he left. Nothing. I don't know what I did to make him fall out of love with me or what made him go wandering. And the hardest part is that he turned his back on his daughter. I understand falling out of love with his wife, but to turn his back on his own flesh and blood. I just can't come to terms with that."

"That really does surprise me. It just doesn't sound like the Justin I know. You two always seemed to be so happy together."

"That's just it! I thought we were too. If we had been arguing with each other, having disagreements, I could understand his being disgruntled and beginning to look elsewhere for love. But nothing."

Sadie contemplated what to say next very carefully to avoid hurting Jackie's feelings. "Jackie, I know it's been a long time since we've seen you two. Why didn't you come home more often?"

Jackie looked at her in surprise. What did this have to do with her dilemma now? "We were just too busy, I guess. Jesse had become a teenager and was involved in things in her life. I was busy with my group of charities, and Justin was tied up with work. Justin took on another class to teach, and, well, there just didn't seem to be time. Why do you ask about that?"

"It's just that Mom and I discussed on several occasions how long it had been since you had come home for a visit, and even though Mom and Dad went down to Texas to visit you a couple of times, the rest of us really missed you. And you and I have not spoken to each other in a long time like we used to. To tell you the truth, I was beginning to wonder if I'd done something to make you upset with me, and that was why you didn't come home. I thought maybe you didn't want to see me."

"Oh, Sadie, that's not true! Not at all. I'm so sorry you got that opinion."

"Mom couldn't understand it either. She's been worried about you for quite some time, even if she wouldn't talk with you about it. We were also afraid something was going on in your family you didn't want us to know."

"Not at all. Oh my God! I can't believe this! I've never felt that way at all about the family. That's why I came home. I knew I could count on my family to be here for me when I needed them. Where else could I turn for help? You all are my life." Tears stung her eyes as she contemplated how she'd hurt her family unknowingly.

"I didn't mean to make you cry. Oh, Jackie." Sadie rose and went around the table to wrap her arms around her sister. "You know we will all be here for you. You can come to us anytime you want, and I'm truly happy you decided to come home. We just couldn't understand why you were distancing yourself from us, that's all."

"Honestly, I didn't realize I had been doing that."

"Could this have anything to do with what happened between you and Justin, do you think?" Sadie asked.

This really surprised Jackie. "What do you mean? I don't get your drift."

"It's just that, over time, maybe you two changed. You said you've all been so busy—Justin with work, you with charities, and Jesse with whatever it is teens do these days. Could you have just become so wrapped up in yourselves that you neglected to nurture the love you have for each other?"

This was a new thought to Jackie, one she had never contemplated before. She bit her lip considering this possibility. Yes, she could see how that could have happened.

"I never thought …" began Jackie. "I just never considered that … I mean, do you really think that was the problem?" She let out a deep sigh. "You know, we really did change. I think you're right. Now that I think about it, not only did we stop coming home to visit, but we also stopped doing things for, and even with, each other. I think I was so busy with Jesse and her life, and then my meetings and agenda for first one thing and then another, I was neglecting Justin."

"Whoa, I didn't say this was your fault," Sadie said. "What about Justin? Did he make dates with you? Send you messages during the day that he missed you? Did he bring home flowers?"

"You're right. We were both at fault. I think we just got so wrapped up in living that we both sort of forgot about each other. Oh, we poured our hearts and souls into Jesse, or at least I did. I thought Justin did too.

But he and I just sort of became roommates. The romance just seemed to vanish. I don't know when or how it happened. But we stopped thinking about each other and what was important to the other one. How do people allow that to happen to their marriage?"

"Love is something that doesn't grow unless you nurture it. You have to keep thinking of your mate. Do you remember when you were newly married? What kind of things did you do to please Justin?"

"Well, at least once a week, I would fix his favorite dish, chicken pasta in a garlic basil sauce, a dark-leafed salad with roasted red pepper Italian dressing. And I would massage his feet after his shower if he'd been on his feet a lot during the day. I haven't done that in years."

"You see, that's what I'm talking about. Those little things are what really add up in a marriage. They are like the little stitches that hold the entire piece of clothing together. By themselves they don't seem like much, but if you put them all together, they really hold the marriage together."

Jackie continued to reminisce. "I remember when Justin would bring home a bottle of champagne, have it chilling on ice, and have the lights turned down low with soft music on for me when I'd get home late."

"And now that you think about it, you miss it, don't you?"

"Yes, I really do."

Sadie went on. "And let me guess. You both just got so busy that slowly, over time, both of you quit doing those little things for each other. Right?"

"That must be it. For the last several years, it seemed like there was never enough time. We were always rushing here or hurrying to get there on time. The pace of life around San Antonio is … well, just fast. You get so caught up in it that you forget how slow life can be, like around here. There really was no time for family life of any kind. I would call it the proverbial rat race.

"Maybe that's why I wanted to come home. I felt like I was one of those mice running around and around on the treadmill, and I just needed to get off. Maybe deep down I knew I could get my bearings back if I just came home, so I could step back from the way I'd been living and take a good, long, hard look at things, reevaluate things to see what is truly important to me."

27

Sadie smiled. "Now that's my old sister talking, not the one who was always talking about her charity dinner she was planning or the benefit dance for someone else. I suppose it's good to be busy with something, especially helping people, but it should be kept in its place and never be allowed to override the really important things like family."

"Yes, I can see that now." Jackie sighed. "But I'm afraid it's too late now. Justin's gone forever, and I've learned a bitter lesson too late."

"Oh, you don't know that. Whatever prompted him to leave might not end up being so important to him after all. Give it time. Wait and see what happens."

"You sound just like Mom and Dad." Jackie laughed.

Chapter 5

Jesse and Jackie headed out bright and early Tuesday morning for Jackie's grandparents' home, an hour away from her parents' home, wearing their old jeans and T-shirts, ready for work.

After visiting the Craigs for a while, Jackie said, "Well, Mom said you have some windows that need washing, and as you can see, we're dressed for work. So point me in the right direction, and we'll get started."

Grandma Craig said, "Oh, honey, you don't need to come here and work like that. Mac down the road does odds and ends for us. I know he'll be glad to do them."

"But he'll want to be paid, right?" Jackie asked.

"We give him something for his trouble," she replied.

"Then Jesse and I insist. We don't mind. Let us do this for you. We've been gone for so long and haven't been able to do anything for you. Please let us do this."

"Well," Grandma Craig said, "if you insist. The bucket's on the back porch along with some rags in it. And you can poke around under my kitchen sink and see what you can find to use to wash them with. I keep the vinegar in the pantry."

"Vinegar?" asked Jesse. "What's that for?"

Jackie laughed. "Grandma does things the old-fashioned way, Jess. A little vinegar and dishwashing soap, and you've got a good window-washing fluid."

"Bet it smells real good," Jesse said as she got up to go in search of the bucket.

They washed all the windows in record time, thankful the house was not two stories tall, even though the windows were extremely long, reaching nearly to the floor. But with Jesse working inside and Jackie outside, together they worked their way around the house and were finished by midafternoon.

After they were done, they fixed themselves iced tea. Jesse said to Grandma Craig, "So I understand Mom is named after you."

"That's right."

"So tell me," Jesse said, looking at her mom, "how do you feel about your name?"

Grandma Craig looked at Jackie. "Well, I'm really like your mama. I don't like my name very much either, but I guess I'm stuck with it. I've carried it for eighty-five years. I guess I can carry it the rest of my time on this earth. I just never had the opportunity to get rid of it like your mama. Who cares what your name is anyway? What's more important than what you're called is what comes to people's minds when they speak of you. What kind of a reputation have you built up over the years?

"For instance, what would you like people to think of when they say Jesse Jacobs?"

"I guess I'd like for them to think well of me, to have good thoughts of me."

"Then the important thing is for you to live your life in such a way that people will think of you in a good way when your name comes up."

"Is that how people think of you, Grandma?" she asked.

"I'd like to think so. I've made a lot of friends over the years. People from all around know who we are and know we'd do anything for any of them if they needed help. Lord knows we've done a lot for the folks around here."

"Like what?" prompted Jesse.

"Well, I've helped in birthing the babies around the countryside. Back in our day, the hospital was a long way off, and getting there by horse and buggy was risky business, especially in the snow and ice. Oh, some folks had automobiles, but not many. Anyway, it was usual for neighbor women to help each other if there weren't doctors. And we live five miles away from a town, so by the time someone went for a doctor, because not many had telephones back then either, why, the baby would most likely be born already by the time the doctor arrived.

"Then your grandpa has helped all the farmers with their crops, especially if the weather didn't cooperate and they had to get the crops in before winter. There was one time Conroy Ames, down the road, got hurt real bad, and all the farmers around chipped in and helped gather his crops in for him, on top of getting their own crops in. That was a hard time, a lot of long days, because back then, very few had tractors, so it was done by horse-drawn machinery. But they all worked together, and it finally got done, but the snow was flying before all the crops were gathered that year.

"There was also the grip, as we used to call it. Today you call it pneumonia. If someone was too bad to take care of their young'ns, we'd pitch in and do laundry and cooking for them. It was a real bad thing, the grip. Could kill you easy as pie.

"But listen to me goin' on. You don't care about what happened back then. I guess I just got carried away reminiscing."

"No, Grandma, it's really interesting. I like hearing about when you were young. Tell me how you and Grandpa met."

Grandma Craig chuckled before answering. "Well, there wasn't much opportunity to meet boys back then, like now. We didn't have a car; they were just becoming popular, but mostly in the cities. Us country folk, well, we were still driving horse and buggy long after city folk had cars. Anyway, as I was saying, there wasn't much opportunity to meet boys. But our churches would have socials, as we called them. They were gatherings usually in summers, on the church property, where folks from all around could come and socialize. Well, I had gone with Mama and Papa to a social at our church, and I happened to turn around and was staring into the blackest eyes I'd ever seen before. It was your grandpa, and he was staring right back at me." She let out a giggle upon remembering it.

Jackie and Jesse looked at each other and smiled. "Anyway," Grandma Craig went on, "the rest is history."

"So, how long did you date, and where did you get married?" Jackie asked.

"Oh, we dated, as you call it, for about a year before tying the knot. But when we got together back then, it wasn't a date like you call it today. John would come up to spend the day here at the house. We didn't go anywhere. Sometimes his folks would invite our family down to their house for the day. But we didn't get to be together as often as the young ones do today because, even though he only lived about twenty miles away, it took about two hours to get there by horse and buggy. And if you lived on the farm like we both did, there were so many chores to be done that there just wasn't much time for having fun visiting all over the countryside.

"We got married at our church here, and Mama and Papa invited everyone to come to their house afterward for cake and coffee. We lived with Mama and Papa for a time, until we found a place of our own. Things are sure different today, aren't they?"

Jesse looked at her mother. "I'd really hate to have to live with my parents after getting married."

"Well, we didn't know any better then. We were just happy to be together finally."

This hit a sore spot with Jackie, who rose and declared it was time for them to be heading home.

"It sure was nice to have you two come down for the day. And if you don't have anything to do later on, the blackberries are coming on early this year. I'm afraid they'll be ready to pick in a couple of weeks. I sure could use the help putting them up."

Jackie bent to kiss Grandma Craig on the cheek and told her they'd be glad to help her. Maude would call her when the berries were ready and see when they could come.

The truck loaded with all their possessions arrived on Thursday at the storage unit Jackie had procured, ready to be unloaded by Jackie, Jesse, Richard, and his two sons, Travis and Drew. She thanked God Sadie had boys. With all the help, it didn't take long to get it all out of the truck and into the storage unit on Saturday, which left Sunday for family association again.

Jackie noticed how Jesse had grown very fond of Travis's two kids, Jacob and Sadie. It seemed to bring out the motherly instinct in her, and she never seemed to mind taking them for walks around the block, rocking Sadie to sleep, or swinging Jacob on the backyard swing. She would read books to Jacob when it was his nap time, and Travis commented how much Jacob looked forward to being with Jesse. Jackie was happy that Jesse was having this opportunity to get to know her family so well.

After everyone left for home that Sunday evening, Jackie, Jesse, and the Righters sat on the front porch. Jesse said, "So, Grandma, if Mom is named after Great-grandma Craig, is Sadie named after someone?"

"Why, yes," she answered. "That's your great-grandma Righter's first name. Do you remember them? I bet not. They've both been dead for a long time."

"No," Jesse answered, "I don't. Where did they live?"

"Well, you know I was raised on the farm where my parents still live, and Don came from a little town just east of there, called Westhaven, not much more than a spot in the road. That's where they lived."

"Then how did you and Grandpa come to live here in Stoner?"

"Well, shortly after we were married, Don got a job in a machine shop here. We were married in 1963, and we moved up here in '64. I was pregnant with Sadie when we moved. We found a little apartment down on Main Street over the hardware store. Anyway, Don went to work for old Mr. Lowry in the machine shop, and when he retired, Don was able to buy the shop. It's hard to believe that he's now planning on retiring and selling the shop. It's made a good living for us over the years, thankfully. But I guess it's time for someone younger to take over.

"Then," she went on, "when Mrs. Slaughter died and this house went on the market, I just had to have it. Poor Don couldn't see how we could afford it, but Mom and Dad loaned us the down payment, and we bought it. That was the year after your mom was born. It would have been 1968. We paid all of $9,000 for it. He now calls it the Beast, although I think he means it in an affectionate way," she said with a twinkle in her eye.

Jesse had more questions than an attorney in a court of law. She asked Rose,

"So what was it like to grow up on a farm?"

Rose contemplated this. "It was really good. We had a lot of work to do—cows to milk, chickens to feed, sheep to feed—all before going to school. But I had three brothers and two sisters, you know, to help, so we'd fly into the barn and hurry as fast as we could so we could be done and ready for school in time to hitch a ride with a neighbor.

"They say our neighbors thought we were rich because of all the land my parents owned, but I didn't ever feel like we were. We had food on our plate and a good roof over our head, but if Dad wasn't as handy as he was, that might not have been the case. I was always glad my parents taught us the value of hard work. Kids these days don't have the chores we did back then, and I think they seem lost, with nothing to do, so they get into trouble. Maybe if people would leave the cities and go back to living on farms where there's always hard work, and plenty of it, our kids would grow up to be better fit for adulthood.

"But listen to me ramble on. Anyway, the next time you go visit Mom and Dad, have him tell you about what all he's done to their house while they've lived there."

There was silence for a few minutes before Rose continued. "But there was always something to do on the farm other than work too. We always had a couple of horses to ride, the woods to explore, the pond to swim in, the barn to play in, and usually company on the weekends. I remember my childhood with fond memories." She seemed to be off in her own world as her memories came flooding back from the distant past.

"I think I would have liked to have grown up on a farm like that," admitted Jesse.

Jackie said, "Jesse! I thought you were happy in Texas. I thought you rather liked the city life."

"Oh, I do. I just thought it would be nice to be able to live on a farm too. Wouldn't it be nice to grow up in both worlds? How can a person do that?"

They laughed. "You'd have to live half your life in one place and half in the other," offered Rose.

"You said your neighbors thought you were rich, but you didn't think you were?" Jesse inquired.

"Well," Rose answered, "I wouldn't say rich. Comfortable maybe. Mom and Dad didn't buy all their land; they inherited some of it from

Dad's parents. But they were frugal with their money and eventually were able to purchase more farm ground. They were wise with their money and didn't spend it on things like cars or other luxuries. Oh, don't get me wrong. They did finally break down and buy a car, but that's the car they still have, a 1936 Chevy coupe, which he picked up in 1945, after being discharged from the army. He got it used from an old woman who hardly ever drove it. Have you seen it?"

"No," answered Jesse.

"Well, that doesn't surprise me. It's in the toolshed, rotting away. They gave up driving about five years ago, but they won't sell the car. They're afraid they might *need* to go someplace. It doesn't matter that neither of them have driver's licenses anymore. If they really needed to go someplace, I know they'd call Mac down the road from them. He's their right-arm man. Anyway, the old car doesn't even have a back seat anymore. I doubt it even runs. I suppose some collector might be willing to give good money for it, though, since it's sat in that toolshed protected from the elements, and he took really good care of it when he was younger, so it has no rust on it."

"Wow!" Jesse said. "Can you imagine an old car like that just sitting there? It's probably worth a fortune."

Jackie laughed. "I doubt a fortune but probably a good amount if you could find the right buyer. However, we probably won't know until they're both gone."

Jackie said to Rose, "Grandma asked us to come back and help her when it's blackberry-picking time, and I told her we would."

Chapter 6

The next two weeks were spent poring over the newspapers for job opportunities for Jackie and Jesse. Jesse had decided she'd get a job for the summer before school started, and she was able to obtain a position working at the town library part-time for the summer. Jackie, on the other hand, was beginning to worry that she couldn't seem to find anything suitable. She felt it was her own fault, though, that she didn't have a work history and references. She'd gone to college, but after the birth of Jesse, she'd decided to stay home until the children they would have were all in school. However, there never were any more children, and by the time Jesse had entered school, she was busy with her charity work, which she'd found quite enjoyable. They also had decided they didn't need another income—another reason she'd never gone to work. And by working voluntarily for charities, she'd been free to run after Jesse and become more involved with her school's extracurricular activities. She had never regretted forgoing work in order to be there for Jesse—until now. However, if she had it all to do over again, she knew she'd do the same thing. She would just have to convince someone to take a chance on her abilities.

Eventually, the time came for her and Jesse to go to the Craig's to help pick blackberries. Jackie waited until Friday, the day Jesse had off from work, and decided to spend the weekend at the Craig's house.

Jackie tied her hair back with a bandana and encouraged Jesse to do the same because of the heat. Thankful that the blackberries were the domestic kind, without thorns, they diligently began picking around ten and didn't finish until noon. Wet from perspiration and

Jackie complaining from a backache, they took five gallons of berries into the house. Grandma Craig had two glasses of iced sweet tea ready for them. Jackie preferred her tea without sugar, but she wasn't about to complain. They both dropped into chairs at the kitchen table. Jesse promptly downed the entire glass and held it out to Maude for another.

"I swear, Grandma," began Jackie, "I don't see how you've done that all these years. That kills your back to be bent over like that for so long."

"You get used to it," Maude said. "You're just not used to it. Now this afternoon, we can begin making jelly, and we can make some pies to freeze."

Jackie and Jesse stole a look at each other, Jesse rolling her eyes in disbelief. Maybe she didn't want to live on a farm after all.

However, after they'd had a sandwich, Grandma Craig insisted they both go shower before beginning work in the kitchen. Afterward, they both felt refreshed and ready to dig in on the berries.

Jesse began washing the berries, while Jackie began making pie crusts. Grandma Craig stayed in the living room cutting squares of cloth to make a quilt top. It had become difficult for her to stand for long periods on her feet, and cooking had all but become obsolete in her kitchen. Jackie was glad she could assist her, even if it was only in this small way. At least Grandma Craig would be able to thaw a pie and pop it in the oven when company came to call. Grandma Craig could still be a hostess without too much work involved.

Jesse and Jackie could hear Grandpa's ball game on the television as they worked, but they could also hear him snoring. They were able to put five unbaked pies in the freezer before three o'clock and had begun a batch of jelly when Maude came to see how things were going for them. She lowered herself into a chair at the table to chat while they worked. Jelly was one thing she wasn't leaving entirely up to Jackie because she wasn't sure Jackie had ever made jelly, and if it wasn't cooked just right, or if she neglected to add enough sugar, it wouldn't turn out right.

As they began to work on the jelly, Maude asked Jackie, "So, how are things at Rose's? Are you two getting adjusted to life in the North?"

Jesse told her about her part-time job three days a week at the library, for which Maude praised her. Jackie's news at not having landed any work made Maude reassure her that she was certain she would find something. Then Maude asked her, "Have you heard from Justin?"

Jackie quit stirring the berries. "No, but then I didn't really expect to."

"Well, these things take time, you know," Maude added. "I remember when …" She abruptly stopped talking, causing Jackie and Jesse both to turn to look at her.

"When what?" Jackie asked.

"Oh, I probably shouldn't say anything. It's in the past anyway."

"No, really, I want to know. When what?" she asked again.

"Well …" Maude paused. "I remember when, well … Oh, I don't know if I should say. Your mother said she was never going to tell her girls."

This really intrigued Jackie. She took her pan of berries off the burner and gave her entire attention to Maude. "Tell her girls what?"

"Well, if you must know. I really think it's something you should know about because of what you're going through right now."

"What should I know?" insisted Jackie. "Grandma, tell me."

"I was going to say I remember when your father was unfaithful to your mother, how long it took before they got things patched up."

"What?" Jackie gasped. She was flabbergasted. "Dad? Unfaithful to Mom? No way! This just can't be! I mean … are you sure? When?"

"I probably shouldn't have said anything. But when Rose called me and told me about what happened with you, I asked her if she was going to tell you about herself, and she didn't think it would help anything. But I think it will. I think it will help you to see that it is possible to get back together with your husband and work things out, that it isn't all lost just yet."

Jackie lowered herself slowly into a chair at the table, in shock at this news. Her head was swimming, and she didn't know what to say. How could this be? Her parents had always seemed so happy, so in love with each other. How could she not have known? She could only sit there staring at Maude.

Maude went on. "It was when you were a baby. Don had gotten into the custom of going to a local inn, as he called it, after work, to unwind before going home. I really think it was just a bar, but that's my personal opinion. Anyway, he met someone there, and one thing led to another until … Well, anyway, when Rose found out about it, she packed you girls up and came running down here to us, just like you ran to your mama when you were in trouble. Given time, Don was able to convince her to come back home, and they've been happily married ever since. Thankfully, Don came to his senses, straightened up, left that running around after work, and has been a wonderful husband and father ever since."

"I … I just had no idea," Jackie said. "Why didn't Mom tell me?"

"She didn't want you to look unfavorably toward your father. She knows how much you love your father, and she didn't want to taint the good picture you have of him. And things like that aren't usually talked about. It's over and done with, and Rose feels like it's best forgotten. But I want you to know so you'll see you could quite possibly still have a happy marriage—and for years. You shouldn't be too quick to throw your marriage away because your husband messed up. That's why I wondered if you'd heard from him. I was hoping he'd come to his senses and ask for your forgiveness. And if he should, I hope you will talk things out with him. Try to understand why he did what he did."

Jackie didn't know what to say. She sat there quietly for a while, just trying to sort all this new information out in her head. Her view of her father had always been one of the perfect husband and father. Her view of him was what she had always wanted her husband to be. Now to find out that he wasn't the perfect father she'd always thought he was, well … this was certainly something she'd have to give much thought to. Try as she might, she just couldn't conceive of her mother and father ever being close to a possible divorce.

Maude went on. "I remember the night Don came to talk to Rose. She had refused to speak to him and wouldn't come out of her bedroom. John sat on the front porch talking to him while I was in the bedroom talking to Rose. Don was just sick at heart at how he'd hurt Rose. The remorse he felt was so obvious my heart ached for him, even though I wanted to hit him over the head with my rolling pin for what he'd done to my baby girl. But I knew no good would come of it if they didn't speak to one another. So John and I finally got them together to at least talk. They sat on the porch swing until sometime past midnight. Rose didn't go with him that night, and he didn't stay. But he wouldn't go home without her, he said. So he got a room in town and came back the next morning. They talked again for a long, long time the next day out in the barn.

"When Rose came inside, you could tell she'd been crying. My heart was breaking for her, and it was all I could do not to get involved with the two of them, but I knew the decision had to be made between those two alone about what would become of their relationship. Whatever the trouble between them had to be worked out between them—and them alone.

"Rose packed up you girls and headed home with Don, with reservations about whether she was doing the right thing. She said she'd give it one more try, but she let Don know that if anything like that ever happened again, she'd leave him and never go back to him again. Don knew she meant it. And I don't know any more than that. How rough it was for them to patch up the hurt it caused, only they can answer. But as you know, things seem to have gone well for them ever since, at least from the standpoint of everyone around them."

"So that explains why they both were so insistent that I give it some time."

"I'm certain. Time but also a lot of talking, if he ever should want to try again. And if you should decide to go back to him, you have to, by all means, forgive totally. And that means you can't throw it back in his face again, ever. You will never forget; that's not going to be possible. But you can forgive. Your mother has done a fine job of that, and I would encourage you to try to imitate her attitude if you and Justin get back together."

Jackie swallowed, trying to get rid of the lump that welled up in her throat. She wanted to bury her head in her arms and cry—but not in front of Jesse. She would be strong for her daughter. She took a deep breath, slowly rose from the table, and said, "Jesse, we've got to get this jelly done before tomorrow. I suggest we get busy."

Jesse lit in on mashing the berries but kept her eyes darting to her mother, inspecting her to make certain she was all right.

After they finished the jelly and had them lined up on the cabinet to cool, they melted the wax to pour over the tops before sealing the lids on. They finished just in time to have a BLT for supper. Afterward,

Jackie went out to sit on the porch swing to think about all she'd learned.

What should she do with this new information? Should she let her mother know that Grandma told her? Would her mother be furious with Grandma for telling her? Maybe she should keep this information to herself. Would she look at her father differently now? Would she feel differently toward him?

She began to go over in her mind the kind of man her father was, all the qualities he displayed down through the years. No, she decided. Her father was the man she believed him to be. She knew he had just succumbed to a moment of weakness. He had actually loved her mother all along. He was truly a good man. Hadn't he proved it over the years? Grandma said they'd been happy in their marriage ever since, and hadn't it shown? Yes, she could see how her parents had been able to weather a storm such as that.

But wasn't it different with Justin? He had left her for the other woman, had chosen the other woman over her. Didn't that make a big difference? Didn't that in itself speak volumes as to the kind of man he was? He certainly was not the man her father was. Not by a long shot in her mind. He must not have just fallen because of a weakness. If he had, wouldn't he have stayed with her?

She finally went inside to prepare for bed. She stopped at Jesse's bedroom door to say good night just as she was turning down the covers. "What kind of bed is this anyway?" Jesse asked as she sat down.

"Oh my goodness," Jackie answered as she crossed the room to the bed. She bent to run her hand over the bed. "It's called feather ticking. Looks like Grandma put it on top of the mattress. It's what everyone used to have years ago. I can't believe she still uses feather bedding."

"Will I be able to sleep on this?" she began to lie back, sinking down as the feather ticking enveloped her. She answered her own question, "Oh, yes. This feels so good. You're going to love this, Mom, if it's on your bed too."

Jackie smiled. She remembered taking naps on the feather ticking when she was younger and visited Grandma's house. She'd always loved it and now wondered if she'd sleep at all, with or without the ticking tonight.

Chapter 7

The next morning as Jesse entered the kitchen, Jackie asked how she'd slept on her feather bed. "Wonderful," was the reply. Jackie knew she had slept well because it was already ten thirty, and it wasn't like Jesse to sleep so late. Jesse declared it was the work they'd done the day before that made her sleep in so late, and Jackie readily agreed.

Jesse poured a cup of coffee and sat down at the table, noticing the toaster on the counter with an open jar of their jelly by it. "Did you have some of our jelly?" she asked.

"It is really good. Fix yourself some toast and try it. I think we are so awesome we might just want to go into business making and selling jelly. Do you think we could make enough to live on if we did?" They both snickered.

Maude said, "The next batch of berries will be ready to pick in a few days, but I'll have Mac pick these for me, and he can give them away to some of the neighbors. Lord knows I already have all I want. But the next time you come, I want you to pick some to take to Rose, and be sure to take her a couple of those jars of jelly when you go too."

Jackie thanked her for that. She wasn't sure when she'd be able to come back to pick more berries if she got a job and hoped she would be able to help some more. She wondered how Grandma Craig ever got along without her in the past.

Jesse sat down to the table with her toast in hand and said to Maude, "Grandma said to ask you about what Great-grandpa did to this house."

Just then, John walked into the kitchen with the morning paper in hand. "I'll answer that, if you don't mind, Maude." Then after sitting

42

down to the table, he continued, "When I married Maude, her parents lived here in what was a two-room house. It was what is the living room and front bedroom. The living room was both the living room and kitchen combined. Of course, back then, houses didn't have indoor bathrooms. There was an outhouse at the far corner of the yard, and there wasn't any indoor plumbing. The well is still by the back door, and after getting water piped into the house, we used the well water for the garden, up until we quit putting in a garden.

"As the children came along, we needed more space, so I added a kitchen and dining room and the addition on the side with the hall and three bedrooms. Then in the early fifties, we added the bathroom at the end of the hall and enclosed the back porch to make a utility room. That's when we added the hot water heater, washer and dryer hookups, and furnace with ducts to all the rooms. The air didn't come until the mid-eighties. Oh, yes, and I put new plumbing in the kitchen when we added the bathroom, and before that, about 1945, when we started the construction on the additions to the house, I had the house wired and rewired it again ten years ago. Just three years ago, we replaced the furnace and air with these new energy-efficient kinds."

"Wow! That's a lot of work. Did you have plans or just figure out what you wanted to do and just did it?"

"That's right. We didn't feel we could afford an architect and all that. My brothers and father helped with things I couldn't do alone, until we all became too old to do anything anymore. Anyway, over the years, it all got done. Back then, if you wanted something done, you pretty much had to do it yourself, or have someone offer to help who knew what to do if you didn't. That's where family comes in really handy."

"Grandpa, can I ask you something else?"

"Sure."

"Well, I noticed that part of your fingers are curled closed. Were you born that way, or did something happen to you?"

"I got burned in a fire when I was still a newlywed. One night in a bad storm, lightning struck our barn and burned it to the ground. I tried to save as many animals as I could, but we still lost a horse and two cows. Anyway, I got burned, and this is the result," he said, holding his hand up. "Even though it's my right hand, the hammer fits just right in it, and I was able to rebuild that barn across the way after I got healed up—with help, of course. You know, they couldn't do things for people who got hurt back then like they can today. I didn't even go to a hospital. The closest one was at least forty miles away. But you know what? This hand never did stop me from doing anything I set my mind to."

John asked Jesse if she'd ever been fishing, to which she informed him she had not. They agreed on taking a walk down to the pond in the pasture after Jesse got ready and had dug a few worms out of the backyard, from the little garden plot that had two tomato vines. Jackie declined going, saying she had her mind set on washing some curtains instead.

By noon, Jackie had the first batch hanging on the line in the back of the house and another batch in the machine. By the time Jesse and John arrived with a string of fish, Jackie and Maude were cutting squares from material and sewing the quilt top together.

Jesse was excited about fishing, declaring she liked it very much. However, she was dismayed when John said anyone who fished also had to help clean them. She reluctantly followed him to the backyard. Afterward, she stated that she never wanted to go fishing again. That brought a round of laughter from everyone.

"You won't feel the same way after tasting them tonight," John declared. "Maude has a beer batter recipe for fish that will change your way of thinking about that. Guaranteed!"

"Well, we'll see about that," she countered, after which she promptly excused herself, saying she was in much need of a shower to get the fish smell off her.

When she returned, she noticed the quilt for the first time and said, "What a neat quilt this will be when it's done."

Maude said, "It's called the wedding ring pattern. I'm making it for Douglas's granddaughter. I don't suppose you know them, do you?"

"Who's that?" she asked.

"Douglas is your grandma Rose's older brother by two years. His granddaughter is getting married in a few months and mentioned she'd like to have one of my quilts. It's not as easy for me to make anymore, but I told her mom I'd try. Do you have one of my quilts, Jackie?"

"No, but I figured someday I'd have one of yours that Mom has."

"Well, no reason you shouldn't have it right now. Jesse, there's a step stool folded up by the refrigerator. Go get it and get up in the door above my closet door. They're all stored up there, and your mom can pick which one she wants."

Soon, the battered fish had been eaten, along with baked potatoes and salad, and more iced tea was poured. Jackie took her glass and headed for the porch with Jesse on her heels. They sat in silence for a long time while nighttime slowly descended, bringing out the lightning bugs. Eventually, the bullfrogs by the pond's edge began to send their songs out over the gentle breezes of the evening. The summer was fast becoming hotter, which Jackie knew would end in what they used to call the dog days of summer, when it was so hot you could fry an egg on the cement walk, and a person's strength was sapped right out of them so that it took real effort just to move. How had she ever survived the humidity there when she was small, especially without air-conditioning? Shortly after dark, the mosquitoes seemed to arrive en masse, driving Jackie and Jesse back inside.

Sunday dawned sunny and very warm. After breakfast, made up of juice, pancakes, and eggs, Jackie began hanging the already washed and dried curtains and washing more. She would have to gauge her work carefully so she could hang the freshly washed ones after drying on the line, because she wanted to get back to her mom's house by dark.

Rose asked Jackie if she would mind running into town and getting a few things at the grocery store before she left, and she gladly accepted. She and Jesse left with the list in hand and returned an hour and a half later.

Jesse said to Rose as they came in, "Mom was hit on in the parking lot of the store."

"What?" Rose responded. "Someone hit your car?"

"No, she was hit on. You know, a guy asked for her phone number."

Rose still wasn't getting it. "What on earth are you talking about?"

"A man wanted to ask Mom out on a date."

"Oh, that's what *hit on* means these days." Rose chuckled. "I thought someone hit her or hit your car." They laughed.

"Jesse," Jackie said, "he was only being kind." Then she turned to Rose. "I dropped some things out of my bag when it ripped. He stopped to help me pick things up."

"And," Jesse said, "men don't ask for phone numbers of someone they are just *helping*, as you say." Then to Rose, she said, "He wanted to know her name and number, and it wasn't because of a car wreck. We'll see if he was just being kind. I bet he calls for a date." She began taking things out of the grocery sack. "What will you tell him if he calls?"

"I will tell him to get lost—in a kind way, of course."

"Good," Jesse said. She certainly didn't want anything to come between her mom and dad if there was a possibility they could get back together. "Besides, he isn't nearly half as good-looking as Dad."

"That certainly sounds like a prejudiced remark," Jackie said.

"Well, it's true."

Jackie knew the man was very interested in her but wasn't about to let on to Jesse. Her sack had ripped in the parking lot of the store, causing several canned goods to roll out onto the pavement. The man had been at her side in an instant to help retrieve them. Then he said, "You must be new around here. I've never seen you before. Hi, my name is Ken Foltz." Jackie had introduced herself and Jesse to him, letting him know they were not from around the area but were visiting family. He had asked who her family was and assured them he knew her grandparents well and liked them. Jackie had looked him over carefully then, not certain about why he had wanted to know about her family. He seemed too friendly for someone who just happened by just when her sack had torn. Then he had asked if she was going to be in town for a while, to which she had answered no, saying she was leaving today. He wanted to know where she was from, and she asked him why he wanted to know. He looked down at his shoes, paused, and then asked for her phone number. She knew then he wanted to get to know her better. Had she been out of the dating scene so long that she'd forgotten a come on when she was faced with one? Then she realized she no longer wore her wedding band, having removed it as soon as Justin left. Her thumb instinctively felt for the missing ring. So he had noticed she wasn't wearing a band and had assumed she wasn't married.

She had told him she saw no reason to give him her number, since she wasn't from there and would be leaving anyway. He had asked if she'd be coming back, to which she'd replied, "Probably someday." He then said he'd still like to have her phone number and would like to show her around if she came back to town. She quickly rattled off her cell number, hoping he'd realize it was a Texas number, realizing his inquiries were pointless. Then she quickly excused herself, got her bags loaded in the trunk of the car, and took off as quickly as she could.

Jesse kidded her all the way home about the man—Ken. Even though she knew her mom would never even look at another man but her dad, still it was strange to see someone trying to get a date with her. Jackie had warned her not to breathe a word of it to anyone, but of course, Jesse had no intention of obeying and blurted it all out the minute she got in the door.

That evening on the way back to Don and Rose's house, her cell phone rang. Her heart leapt into her throat with the thought that it could be Justin. However, upon answering it, she found it was Ken. She was let down. He had called to see if the number she'd given him really was her number, she figured. How did he remember it? She'd rattled it off so fast she was certain he would forget it immediately.

"So, are you headed back to Texas today?" he asked.

"Not exactly." She hoped she sounded vague.

"Look, I'm sorry if I came on too strongly today," he continued. "But I was hoping we could get to know one another. I was going to ask you out if you hadn't been leaving right away."

"That's nice," Jackie said while glancing at Jesse. She hoped Jesse would not be able to ascertain who was on the other end, and she was being as elusive as possible so she wouldn't figure it out.

"Do you think you'll be coming back to visit the Craigs any time soon?"

"I really couldn't say."

"Well, I couldn't help but notice that you're not wearing a wedding ring, and I just thought maybe you'd … uh … Look, let me tell you a little about myself so you won't be too afraid to get involved with me. I have a construction company here in town, and I have a good reputation. I've been in business for seventeen years. I'm known all over these parts, and I do quite well. I've been married once, but my wife died five years ago. I won't beat around the bush. I'm looking to get married again. When I saw you in the store lot, with your canned goods rolling all over, well, I just couldn't help myself. Then when I didn't see a ring, my hopes shot up that maybe ... Well, may I at least leave you my phone number so you can call me if you do come back to town soon?"

"I guess that would be fine."

He gave her the number and said he hoped she would be coming back soon and that she would call. She said goodbye and hung up, with no intention of remembering the number or calling it. She had gotten rid of him, and that was all she cared about. Jesse asked her who it was, and Jackie said it wasn't anyone important.

"It was him, wasn't it? That Ken guy at the store," Jesse said. "Why did you give him your phone number if you're not interested in going out with him?"

"I really didn't think he would remember it. I said it so fast. I was just trying to get away from him as quickly as I could."

"Well, that's great! Just great! Now he'll probably bug you to death since he remembered your number."

"Jesse, you know I have no intention of going out with him. Stop worrying about it. He won't know when we're back at Grandma's house, and I'll never see him again. He certainly got no indication from that phone conversation that I was interested in furthering a relationship with him. Don't you agree?"

"But that doesn't mean he won't keep trying. That doesn't mean he won't keep calling you."

"Well, he can try all he wants. It won't do him any good. And now that I have his number in my cell phone's recent call list, I don't have to answer the phone if he does keep calling me."

That night before retiring, Jackie stood for a long while, looking at her image in the mirror. She was almost forty years old. Could she still be attractive to men? Or perhaps had Ken only been interested because she was someone new in the area? He said he was well known, which meant he knew everyone as well, so there probably wasn't anyone who lived around there that he wanted to date. And there probably weren't that many his age to choose from anyway. She turned from side to side and wasn't unhappy with what she saw. She pulled her hair back from her face and studied it. Still, she wasn't unhappy with the image staring back at her in the mirror. Oh, yes, she had a couple of very small lines at the corners of her eyes, the beginnings of crow's feet. But her complexion was smooth and even, and her features were well proportioned. She had her mother's nose, straight with a slight turn upward at the end and rather pointed. Her father had told her once she had the nose of an aristocrat. Her eyes were a soft blue, as her father's were, but large like her mother's. She had inherited her dimple in her right cheek from her grandpa Righter. But since she didn't remember him, she had to take that on the word of the family. She had always been glad to see the mix of both her parents in her. She had to admit, though, that she had more Craig in her than Righter. Nothing she was ashamed of at all.

She inspected her body once again. Was it showing signs of aging? Not really, she decided. She still had a flat stomach, and her buttocks were not sagging. She chocked this up to her tennis, swimming, bicycling, and family basketball when Jesse needed to practice when she was on the team at school, before she'd become a cheerleader. Jackie never was one to sit down and do sit-ups, leg raises, and all that, but she loved sports and participated regularly in them. The only thing she attributed to age was the backache she'd acquired picking berries, but that probably had more to do with the position she had to be in for two hours than age. After all, didn't Jesse complain? And she was only seventeen. She decided she didn't look that bad, but that didn't mean she had any desire to get involved with another man. She just wanted to look good for … well, for herself.

She fell asleep while contemplating spending the rest of her life alone, without a man. Did she really want to do that?

Chapter 8

Jesse enjoyed her work checking out books for people and restocking the shelves when they were checked back in. There were days she wasn't really busy and was allowed time off to go to a store or just to look around.

One day she came home all excited. "Guess what!" She rushed inside, throwing her purse down on the chair as she entered. "You'll never guess!"

Grandpa Don said, "I'll bet you're going to tell us whether we want to hear it or not."

Jesse went on without acknowledging the barb. "Guess who came into the library today?"

Jackie stopped looking at the classifieds, lowered the paper, and asked, "Who?" because she couldn't imagine who Jesse knew in town. Then just as Jesse began, Jackie remembered, and both she and Jesse said at the same time, "James Talbot."

They laughed, and Jesse said, "Yes, and know what? I have a date with him this Friday night. What do you think of that?"

"Awfully fast, don't you think?" remarked Don, pretending to still be reading his section of the paper but with a smile on his face. He knew full well how things worked these days, because of how quickly his grandsons had married. He figured this was the beginning of the end of Jesse's childhood. "He hasn't come to ask my permission yet."

"Oh, Grandpa," grumbled Jesse. "He said he remembers me from way back when I was a kid visiting here, and he always wondered what had happened to me. I didn't think he'd even noticed me."

"So, he's still around here, huh? Well, now you know," Jackie said.

"Well, he's here at least for the summer. He's going to the U of I and will be leaving this fall again. He said he has two more years to go. He's studying to be a computer programmer."

"So he's going to be like all the rest of the kids today who go to school, get out, and can't find a job, is he?" Grandpa asked.

Jesse gave him a smirk, showing her displeasure at his teasing. "Now when he comes by Friday to pick me up, you be nice to him, Grandpa."

Don gave Jesse a look of shock. "Me? But, of course, I'll be nice to him, as long as he's nice to you. But if he should do something foolish with you, you just let him know he'll have the wrath of your grandpa to contend with."

They all chuckled. Jesse bounded up the stairs two at a time, and Don said, "You've got a really fine girl there, Jackie. You and Justin have done a good job of raising her. You should be proud."

"Oh, I am, Dad. Very proud. I just hope she ends up marrying a boy who loves her more than anything else in the world and who will always take good care of her."

"That's what every parent wants for their kids," Don commented. Then looking at Rose, he asked, "Have I always taken good care of you, honey?"

"Always," Rose replied as she puckered for a quick peck.

Jackie couldn't help but wonder at how much in love they still seemed to be after what Grandma Craig had told her. She wanted to see if they would talk about their past troubles, so she asked, "How many years is it now that you two have been married?"

Rose answered, "Forty-three years come September."

Jackie said, "So, how have you two stayed so happily married all these years?"

Rose looked at Don before answering. "You have to decide what you want out of a marriage. We found that if you have the same goals and really work hard to achieve those goals, you'll become more united. It will strengthen the bond between the two of you.

"You can't be happy if one wants a strong relationship with children, but the other one wants to pursue money and doesn't want family responsibilities. Or if one wants to party all the time without giving a thought to family responsibilities, while the other has all the work of trying to keep the family together. It won't work.

"And we've also found that if you have a problem, you talk it out. We've always tried to settle disputes before the day was over. We never aired our differences in front of you girls, but there were times we'd stay up talking long after you were asleep. Because if you don't work out the differences, they will fester until something blows up. That's not good. So it's better to get it out, talk about it, try to fix it, and go on. Right?"

She looked at Don, who readily agreed but then quickly excused himself, saying he had something he was working on in the garage. The conversation had become too intense for him, and he was uncomfortable. If Rose ended up telling Jackie about their troubles when they were young, he didn't want to be involved in the conversation.

However, after he left the room, Rose dropped the subject. Jackie let out a deep sigh. "That's the way it should be, isn't it? It's hard not to talk about things in front of the children, although Justin and I never did have major disagreements of any kind. We always seemed so compatible that way." She seemed to be talking to herself more than to her mother. "Oh, we'd have minor things, like the time I wanted to go skiing in Colorado, and he wanted to go to Hawaii for vacation. But it always seemed we could find a compromise, like with that one. We went the first year to Hawaii and the next year to Colorado. No big deal. You just work it out. Most things just aren't worth fighting about anyway, are they? I mean, unless your husband comes home and tells you he's moving out because of another woman. Now that's one disagreement I was ready to fight over, really have a knock-down drag out. But even with that, he wouldn't fight." With that, she got up and left the room. Rose watched her daughter leave and felt an ache down deep in her soul for her daughter. She knew Jackie was really hurting.

Friday evening arrived, and James came to pick up Jesse at seven o'clock. Don answered the door. They chatted a few minutes, and Jackie and Rose came in from the kitchen to greet him.

Jesse came down the stairs shortly afterward, having heard the doorbell, dressed in white dress slacks, a sleeveless red blouse, and red heels. Don was proud to be her grandfather when he watched her descend the stairs. She was a truly striking young woman. And when he turned to James, he could see he was proud too—proud to have a date with her. It was written all over his face. Don almost laughed out loud.

Don told them to have a good time, but before they could get out the door, he added, "Just make sure you have her back by midnight."

"Oh, Grandpa," Jesse complained.

"I'm sorry, Jesse. That's the rule. There's nothing good that goes on after midnight anyway."

"OK," she said before saying goodbye and giving her grandpa a kiss on the cheek. Don stood on the porch till they drove away, and just as he turned to come back inside, another car drove up in front of the house.

When the man came up the walk, Don examined him closely. He was afraid it was an attorney to see Jackie about a possible divorce Justin wanted. But he determined that the man was too tan to be an attorney. The man had a rugged look about him, not like a pen pusher. But the man did ask if Jackie was home.

After Don called to Jackie and she came out, she looked shocked and said, "Ken!"

He seemed suddenly shy. "Hi," he said.

Don excused himself and went inside. "How did you know where to find me?" Jackie asked.

"Your grandparents gave me the address. I took a chance on you being home. Would you like to go for a drink or something?"

"Thank you, but I don't think so."

"Did I do something to upset you? I didn't mean to. I just thought—"

"No," Jackie interrupted. "Look, won't you sit down?" She motioned to the porch swing. He sat in the swing, and Jackie purposely sat in a wicker chair facing the swing. "I think I should explain something about me."

"I know you're married," he said.

"You do?" She was surprised. "Did Grandma and Grandpa tell you?"

"Yes. And they mentioned that you're separated from your husband, that it was rather recent, and you probably wouldn't have anything to do with me, but they said it wasn't their place to make your decisions, so they gave me your address here. They said I should find out for myself how you felt about dating so soon."

"Well, they're right about that. It has been rather recent, and I just have no desire to get involved with anyone else right now. It really has nothing to do with you personally, you see."

"I can respect that. And even though you're not divorced, still not having your mate around anymore can be really hard to deal with. I know. I've been there."

"Yes, you told me your wife died. I'm really sorry about that."

"Thanks. Anyway, I thought maybe you could use a friend right now. I'm not asking for anything more than that. I just wanted to talk to you and thought maybe you needed someone to talk to as well."

"That's very kind of you. And you drove all the way up here. I'm quite impressed that you'd come so far to see someone you don't even know."

"Well, I didn't have anything else going on anyway. It's a nice night, so the drive was enjoyable. Are you sure you don't want a drink? There's a nice motel with a lounge out by the edge of town."

Jackie laughed.

"Did I say something funny?"

"Oh, no. It's just that there really isn't much around here, is there? I'm from San Antonio, and there are so many places to go. It just struck me as funny that here"—she gestured toward the town—"there really isn't much to do."

"Not much to do unless you're up for traveling a little. I could take you to Champaign/Urbana. That's not too far, and they have more to offer than here. That's for sure."

"No, really. But thanks anyway. Could I offer you a glass of iced tea?"

"That would be nice. Thanks."

Jackie rose to go inside, and Ken stood. She stopped to look at him. It had been a long time since she'd seen a man who rose when a woman did. He was sitting back down when she glanced at him as she opened the screen door.

When she went to the kitchen, her mother wanted to know who the man was. When Jackie explained how she'd met him, Rose said, "It sure doesn't take long before the vultures begin circling, does it?"

Jackie took two glasses of tea to the porch, handed one to Ken, and sat back down.

Ken asked, "So, do you think you and your husband will get back together?"

"I don't know. Right now, it doesn't look like it. But even if we never do, it's still too early for me to ..."

"I know," he said. There was silence for a couple of minutes before he continued. "So you are John Craig's granddaughter. That's funny. I've known the Craigs all my life, and I never knew they had a granddaughter as beautiful as you."

Jackie felt herself blush and lowered her eyes to her hands. Changing the subject, she said, "Tell me, what do you build? You said you have a construction company?"

"Yes." He shifted and crossed his legs to rest one ankle on the other knee. "I do most of my work in Champaign. There's not much going on in Oakley. Most of my work is for commercial buildings, shopping plazas, gas stations, things like that. I used to build homes, but I've found it's hard to please some people. They think they know what they want until you're almost done, and then they come in and change it all around. Then you'd get some man and woman who can't seem to agree on anything, and there'd be almost knock-down drag outs before the house was done. Commercial buildings aren't like that. We work from a blueprint, and rarely are there changes, and when there is, it's usually minor."

He seemed to relax as he spoke of his work, grateful to talk about something important to him. He went on. "The only thing I miss with commercial work is that it is functional, you know, but not really what you'd call beautiful. Anyway, not like a home. Home building can make you feel, I don't know, creative, I guess. But the pay is better with commercial building than with homes. That's for sure.

"But enough about me. What about you? What do you do?"

"Well, I'm looking for a job. I'm afraid I haven't worked since getting out of college years ago, and I'm having trouble finding work because of it. However, I used to be involved in several charities in Texas and volunteered my time for them."

"I could probably use you with my company if you're interested. I need someone to do payroll and things like that in the office. I don't know if you've ever worked with numbers or not. And I'm not a very large company, but I sure could use more help in the office."

"Thank you, but I wanted to stay close to Mom and Dad here."

"Well, if you should change your mind, you've got my number."

She couldn't help but smile at him. He was so cute. And he was trying so hard to impress her. This made her look him over a little more closely. She couldn't help but notice his big arms and well-built chest, which showed through his T-shirt. He was well tanned from being in the sun and had black hair that he wore spiked on the top. It looked as if it would be wavy if allowed to go its own way, but it was held in place with gel, which gave it the wet look. His eyes were blue and sported long black lashes, which Jackie was certain usually got him whatever he wanted as far as women were concerned. She had to admit she liked what she had seen so far, but that didn't change her love for her husband. However, if she were single and looking, she just might look a little closer at him.

"I'm sure you'll find something eventually," he offered. "What kind of work would you like?"

"Anything that will pay the bills," she answered with a chuckle.

"What if I were to set you up so you could work for me, from here. I could get you a laptop, and with networking, you could—"

"Thanks, Ken. I really appreciate what you're trying to do. But I don't think so."

"OK then. At least I tried. Anyway, like I said, if you change your mind.

"Anyway, I'm going to be working all this next week in Champaign, and I have to come this way to go home, so would you mind if I came by next Friday on my way home? Just to see how you're doing in the job market, that is?"

She smiled. "I guess that wouldn't hurt. But I must warn you that if my daughter is home, well … She's not too happy about you. I think she wants her father and me to get back together."

"That's understandable. But just tell her we're friends, nothing more. Maybe I could take you two out for ice cream or something."

"We'll see." Jackie hesitated. "Look, I know I haven't been very friendly. I'm sorry. I just don't want to encourage you in any way to think there could ever be anything between us. I'm not saying my husband and I will get back together. And maybe …"

"I know. Maybe you never will, but it's still too soon. I know. Well, I know what I went through when my wife died. I wanted so badly to be with her, and I couldn't. I know how hard it must be for you, especially since it seems like the breakup wasn't something you wanted. I needed a friend who could understand what I was going through, and I think you need that as well."

Jackie couldn't help but tear up. He was on his knee in front of her immediately, apologizing. "I'm so sorry. I didn't mean to make you … I mean, I just wanted you to know that I am here for you." He took her hand in his and held it, stroking the back of her hand with his thumb.

She swiped at her face, saying, "I know. I'm sorry. I didn't mean to cry. I guess I really am in need a friend about now. My family has been wonderful to me, but they've got wonderful marriages, and I'm not sure they can relate to what I'm going through."

"Exactly. That's what I meant. If you have someone who's been through something similar, they can relate. They know what you're going through. At least you have the possibility of getting back with your husband. That's something, right? You keep thinking about that, and it will lighten your load. And pray about it. It's amazing how much prayer can strengthen you to get through things."

"I know. I do pray."

They talked for a little longer before Ken decided he should probably leave. He promised to stop to see her the following Friday, and as he walked to the edge of the porch, he turned to her and said, "Keep your head up, Jackie. You'll be all right. It might not look like it now, but you'll be fine."

Chapter 9

Don went to the window to peek out to see if Jesse had come home. Jackie looked at her watch and noticed the time. "I really doubt if she'll be home any earlier than midnight, Dad," she commented.

"I know," he said. "But I thought they might have pulled up and were sitting in the car out front the way you used to do." He sat back down to read his book. However, it wasn't five minutes before he was up again, looking out the window.

"Dad, really. Did you do that when Sadie and I went out?"

"You bet I did. And if you hadn't gotten home when you were supposed to, I'd have gone looking for you."

"Really?" she asked. "I had no idea you were such a nervous wreck when we were dating. I'm surprised you didn't have a heart attack." She let out a little chuckle. "Now if it were fifteen after instead of fifteen before, I'd probably be up looking out the window too. But I'm telling you, no kid comes home early from a date, unless the date is a complete flop."

"All the same, it's good to check. Suppose they were out there in the car. I'd want them to see me peeking at them so they wouldn't stay out there longer than they need to. The way I figure it, nothing good comes from being alone in a car.

"You know, your mother and I went out parking one time just to see what all the hype was about. This was after we'd been married for quite some time." He turned from the window to look at Jackie. "It isn't all it's cracked up to be."

Jackie let out a laugh. "Of course not, if you were already married.

Do you think kids really want to be in cars when they're making out? They'd rather be in a bed too, but they're not married yet. Therefore, the car just happens to be the most convenient thing available.

"Anyway, I really doubt that Jesse would go out parking with James on her first date with him. Tonight was probably just a get-acquainted night—lots of talking, you know. At least I hope so.

"Maybe we should have sent you along with them, Dad, as chaperone."

"Not on your life! I've raised my girls. I don't need any more gray hair than I already have." They both laughed.

"I don't know why you stayed up," she went on. "You should have gone to bed with Mom."

"Well, I wouldn't have gone to sleep even if I had." He went to peek out the window again. "Not until everyone is in the house, safe and sound. Why isn't she home yet?"

Jackie checked her watch again. "She still has five minutes, and I can guarantee you she won't pull up till midnight on the nose."

The clock on the mantel ticked away the seconds more loudly than usual, it seemed, probably because Don willed the time to hurry along. It finally chimed midnight, and Don was already up and looking out the window. "So where is she?" he asked.

"Relax, Dad. Give her a few more minutes before you get your panties in such a twist."

At five minutes past midnight, the car pulled up to the curb. Don ran to flip on the porch light to let her know someone was up waiting for her to come inside. Jesse entered the front door soon afterward.

"You didn't make it by midnight" was the first thing out of Don's mouth.

Jesse looked startled. "Gee, I didn't know you meant on the dot."

"Midnight means midnight, not five after."

"Don't fuss too much, honey," Jackie said to Jesse. "He did the same thing to me when I was young. But you should know that in the future, if you don't want to be the cause of a heart attack, you'd better be here on time, not five minutes late."

"So, did you have a good time?"

"Absolutely!" she answered. "We went to a movie and afterward to D&W. We talked and talked about things. He is just like I remembered him."

Jackie smiled that Jesse had found someone she seemed to be happy with. Perhaps this was the real beginning of settling in. Soon Jesse would have more friends, both male and female, she was certain. In the meantime, her job would keep her occupied.

"And aren't you glad he's not pimply faced," Jackie said, and they both laughed, but then remembered they Rose was asleep and tried to stifle it.

They said good night to Don, and everyone went to bed.

The following day, Saturday, dawned sunny and hot. Rose had wanted to work outside in her garden but decided to postpone it till evening when it would begin to cool.

Sadie called to say she was going to Champaign and asked if Rose, Jackie, and Jesse wanted to go along. They made a day of shopping, only looking for Jackie and Jesse, and had lunch together. Even if Jackie felt she shouldn't spend money right then, she knew Jesse had a good time anyway. Sometimes window-shopping was fun, trying on outrageous outfits they knew they never would buy. Sadie was looking for a dress to wear to an upcoming wedding and found just what she wanted before lunchtime.

On the way back home, Sadie remarked, "It really is nice to have you here, Jackie, to go shopping with me. This is the way life should be, doing things with family. I really believe that. Don't you?"

"I have to admit it is something I've really missed. Today was such fun. Thanks for inviting us."

"What was Dad going to do today?" Sadie asked Rose.

"He's trying to finish the birdhouse he's building for the backyard. I told him to take it to the basement to work on it instead of the garage. It's just too hot to be out there."

Jesse asked, "So how long does it stay this hot up here?"

Rose replied, "Oh, it's always hot around the Fourth of July. And it probably won't begin to break till around the end of September or the beginning of October. And then the trees will turn. Have you ever seen the trees in the fall?"

Jesse replied that she had not.

"Then you're in for quite a treat. We'll take you on a drive through the countryside when they're in full color. It is my favorite time of year, I believe. The only problem with it is that it doesn't last long enough.

"By the way, I forgot to tell you, Jackie, that Mom called wondering if you and Jesse would be able to come down this week some time to pick the last of the blackberries."

"Well, now that Jesse is working four days a week, the only time we could go is on the weekend. Maybe we'd better go down tomorrow. What do you say, Jesse?"

"Oh, Mom, I've already told James I'd meet him at D&W tomorrow afternoon—if it's all right with you, that is."

"That's OK. I can go alone, but—"

Sadic interrupted. "I can go with you, Jackie. There's no need to go alone."

"Well, if you want to, but you don't have to."

Jesse said, "But what? You started to say something else"

"Oh, yes. I was going to say, but you'd better make sure you are home when Dad says you're to be home. I wouldn't want you out with James for longer than a couple of hours. So, what time are you supposed to meet him?"

"We agreed on two o'clock."

"That's fine. Then I'll let Dad know you're to be home by four. And you know …"

"I know. Make sure I'm home at four and not a minute after." She rolled her eyes. They all chuckled, and Rose said, "I'm certainly glad I'm not young anymore. Those can be the most stressful years of your life. But, Jesse, if you just remember to do as your mom says, you'll lessen, if not eliminate, most of the problems associated with the teen years."

Jesse agreed that she'd do that, smiling at her mother. She knew she had a wonderful mother. Growing up, she'd known kids who had to pretty much raise themselves, and she'd always been so proud to have a mother who was always involved with her life, education, extracurricular activities, and interests outside of school. If she had to pick the perfect parent to have, she would have picked her mother. She was proud to have such a close relationship with her, another thing most of the girls she grew up with never had. She had always been close with her father as well—and so proud of the fact that she looked so much like him. All her friends in Texas had agreed that he was drop-dead gorgeous, and they acted giddy when he was around. She really missed him.

Jackie said to Jesse, "I'm surprised you are getting with James again so quickly. You just had a date with him last night, and you're seeing him again tomorrow. Isn't that rushing things a bit?"

"Um, maybe," Jesse conceded. "But it's already a week into July, and he says he'll be busy getting ready for school by the middle of August. So, if we're to get to know one another, we've got to use what time we have left of the summer. I'm sure I'll be busy in August, getting ready to go back to school too."

"I guess you're right. Summer is slipping by quickly. And here I was afraid this summer would be boring for you."

Jackie and Sadie headed out to Grandma and Grandpa Craig's house on Sunday. They picked about three and a half gallons of blackberries, which Maude said to give to Rose. Other family members had been there to pick, and this was probably the last picking for the summer, Maude said.

While the girls were picking, Jackie asked Sadie, "Have you ever thought you'd like to live on a farm like this?"

"Not really. I do like to work in the yard though. It's good therapy. When I'm alone outside working, I feel good, like it's where I'm supposed to be. It gives me time to reflect on things, sometimes to work through problems in my mind. But a farm? I think it's more work than I want. Why do you ask?" "I don't know," Jackie answered. "It just seems like every time I come down here, I really like it. The feel of the country, it's so peaceful and quiet. Life seems so different than city life."

"You've been gone too long, Jackie. You've just forgotten what it's really like back here."

"I suppose you're right. But I've visited Grandma and Grandpa before here, and I never felt like I do now on this visit. What's made the difference do you think?"

"Well, before when you'd come for a visit, there would always be lots of family around. It was always so busy when you were here. Now you're coming down when others aren't around. That would certainly make it seem more laid back, easygoing, and definitely different."

"I think you're right. I guess that makes sense. And now I'm involved with actually doing things on the farm—feeding chickens, picking berries, washing windows, and things like that. I can see why Grandma and Grandpa wanted to stay on the farm instead of moving into town. But you know, there's more to it than that, I think. When I'm outside here, I just have to stop and listen. It's really amazing—the sounds during the day as well as night. All I hear in the day is birds and sometimes a chicken or two. And at night, the crickets are so loud, and the bullfrogs down at the pond. It makes me want to sit on the porch all night long. Maybe I'm just getting old. I don't know.

"Jesse even told Grandma and Grandpa how she would have liked to have grown up on a farm. There must be something about the farm that pulls her toward it as well. Of course, part of that is Grandma's stories about what it was like to grow up here on this one. Maybe this is really the way we were all meant to live, instead of all bunched up together in towns. It just seems so much more ..." She paused, thinking of just the right word to use. "Fresh, I think. Clean. Do you know what I mean?"

"Yes, I do. I've always thought of city life as dirty. And the bigger the city, the dirtier. I may live in a city, but it's certainly not big. And I wouldn't want to be in one any bigger than it is."

Grandma and Grandpa thanked the girls for coming and offered for them to stay the night, but they declined, Sadie because she needed to get back for work on Monday morning, and Jackie for Jesse.

However, before they left, Grandpa asked Jackie how the job hunting was going, to which she replied, "Not very well. But I'll keep looking. Something is bound to come up soon."

He seemed thoughtful and then said he might know of something. He'd talk to her about it on her next visit. Soon the girls were headed back to Stoner.

Chapter 10

Monday morning, Jackie went for her jog, which she had begun as a weekday routine shortly after arriving in Illinois. It was a way for her to work not only her muscles but work her mind as well. In the early morning, the grass seemed to glisten with dew. Everything seemed fresh in the early-morning hours, so she would rise shortly after sunup and head out before her parents or Jesse began stirring. The birds were always out en masse in search of their breakfast. Squirrels would be scampering around, burying nuts for their winter stash. The streets were quiet, and sometimes she would be out before the streetlights went off for the day.

This morning, as she headed out, not only was the dew heavy on the grass, but the air was heavy with moisture, causing a white haze to seem to linger in the air. She began her usual jog toward the park but soon had exerted an enormous amount of energy. She realized she had to slow down to catch her breath, and the perspiration dripped profusely. This wasn't exactly fun. The humidity was more than she could bear, so she cut her jog short and headed home.

When she got back, Rose was pouring coffee and asked if she would like a cup. Jackie decided she'd better shower first; she felt so damp. When she came back into the kitchen, Don was reading the morning paper with his coffee. She poured her coffee and sat with them, saying, "I don't see how you can stand the humidity up here. I had trouble breathing out there this morning. It is so bad."

"Usually is bad this time of year, you know. And we've still got August to go. This has been a hotter than usual summer too. Maybe you should think about swimming for exercise. That won't be so hard on you."

"Not a bad idea. I just might do that. Can I have the classifieds?"

Don passed her that section of the paper, and she said, "Grandpa said the next time I come down to visit, he wants to talk to me about some kind of job. What do you suppose that's all about?"

Don lowered his paper enough to look at Jackie. "That's a good question. What would he know of? He doesn't get around much anymore to know who's hiring and who's not. Guess you'll just have to go find out."

Jackie buried her head in the paper's help wanted section, while Rose busied herself with breakfast preparations. Jesse soon floated into the room, ready for work. She grabbed an apple from the refrigerator, bid everyone goodbye, and was out the door.

"Boy, she sure seems to be floating on air," Don commented. "It's amazing what the attention of the male species toward the female can accomplish." Jackie knew he was right.

The week passed quickly, and on Thursday, Jackie decided she should let Jesse know about Ken's promise to stop to see her on his way home from work on Friday. However, before she had the opportunity to breech the subject, Jesse stated that she'd been asked by Michelle if she could babysit for her and Travis on Friday night, so they could go out together. They said it had been a long time since they'd actually had a date, and now that the baby was old enough that they felt comfortable leaving her with someone, they needed time together. Jesse had accepted readily. Jackie was only too happy for her to babysit and decided not to say anything about Ken. Why stir up trouble when she didn't have to?

Ken arrived at Don and Rose's house at seven o'clock Friday evening. When he offered to take Jackie to the ice-cream parlor, she refused. He knew she would but thought he'd try anyway. She asked him if he'd like a glass of iced tea, and he readily accepted. He waited for her to go inside before taking his seat in the swing. They sat on the porch; he was on the swing, and she sat in the same chair as last time, opposite him.

"So, how have you been?" he asked finally.

"I'm doing fine," she answered, although she'd had a very hard day on Wednesday. In the middle of the day, her mind had drifted to

Justin, and she couldn't help but wonder what he was doing just then. As far as she knew, he hadn't taken any extra classes to teach during the summer, but of that she was not certain. Was he teaching right then? Or did he have the summer off, and he was working on building a more permanent relationship with his little bimbo? Was he making love to her right then? Was he whispering in her ear the same expressions of love he used to whisper to her? That's when the tears had begun to fall, and she was unable to stop them. The pain in her heart became overpowering. So she had spent the afternoon in bed and was thankful her parents allowed her the space and privacy to be alone when she needed. They sensed her need, understood it, and busied themselves with their own lives.

"That's funny," he answered.

"What's funny?"

"The way you said that. You sounded like you were trying to convince yourself."

"Well, you may be right about that."

"Can I tell you something?" he went on.

"Sure."

"When Heather died, my wife, I felt exactly like that too. I figured no one wanted to hear about my problems. I figured it would only make everyone around me sad, so I tried to put on a happy face around everyone. But every night, I'd sit on the edge of the bed, staring at the picture of her on the bedstand, and I'd cry. Every night. I wanted so badly for someone to carry my load with me, someone to miss her as badly as I did, someone to cry with. But I don't think anyone could ever miss her the way I did, not even her parents."

"Yeah, I know what you mean." Jackie was amazed at how candid and open this total stranger was with her. He seemed to be able to express exactly how she was feeling. There was silence for a few minutes before Jackie continued. "The bond between a man and wife is too special for anyone else to really be able to understand how it feels to break that bond, unless they've been through it too. But I don't sit and look at Justin's picture at all. That's the last thing I want to see. If I had brought one with me, I'd probably have smashed it by now."

"I can understand that." He was quiet for a few minutes before continuing. "I've never told anyone about that before, about crying every night."

"Your secret's safe with me. Thanks for telling me. If Justin had died, I'm sure I'd have done the same thing. I can't even imagine losing a mate that way."

"She died in a car wreck coming home from work one evening in the rain. They think she lost control of the car on the slick pavement, misjudging a curve, but they're not sure. Anyway, that's how she died."

"I'm so sorry, Ken. Really, I am. That's awful, just awful. Was she killed … I mean … did she die instantly, or did she live afterward for a time?"

"Instantly thankfully. I think it would have torn me up even more if she'd lingered in a hospital, maybe in horrible pain."

"I agree."

There was a long silence, neither knowing what to say next. Finally, Ken said, "Maybe I didn't really want to come to see how you were doing after all. Maybe I was looking for someone I thought could relate to what I've been through, someone I could talk to."

Jackie smiled. She could see this was just as good a therapy for him as it was for her. "I'm glad you feel you can talk to me about it. It must be painful to talk about."

"It used to be. I guess I'm getting used to waking up alone, making my own breakfast and all. It's the night I have the hardest time with. I am so ready to move on with my life. I really hate being alone."

Jackie smiled again. She knew where this was heading and wanted to steer the conversation away from it. They sat in silence, but the silence didn't make her nervous. It was easy to be with Ken. If a man could bare his soul as he had, it closed the gap between stranger and friend. She knew she was beginning to feel Ken was a friend, even if not intimately so.

Ken went on. "There isn't much opportunity to meet women my age. I refuse to find someone in a bar. I don't think she'd be the right material, if you know what I mean. And the only other place I know of to meet someone is in church, and I quit going years ago. Mom was a Baptist, and I just couldn't believe God would torture me in a hell fire for drinking a beer once in a while."

Jackie laughed. "Someone just right will come along someday. Just don't be in such a hurry that you end up marrying someone you aren't really going to be happy with. Don't settle for anything but the best."

He smiled. "That's the way I figure it. That's why I'm here."

"Thank you. I consider that a compliment."

"It was meant as one. Are you certain I don't stand a chance? No, wait! Don't answer that. It took me four years after my wife died before I would even consider looking at another woman. How could I expect you to consider anyone since you've only been separated for—how long?"

"Just a little over three months."

"Exactly. There's no way you're ready to move on. So meanwhile, I guess I'll just have to bide my time here on your porch swing."

They both laughed and then lapsed into silence once more.

Eventually, Jackie said, "So, tell me about the project you're working on now. I assume it's a commercial project."

He explained the construction as a new Walgreens in Urbana. He talked about the exterior being Drive It. Jackie told him she had no idea what he was talking about, so he had to explain that it was a stucco applied in two steps, with a colorant added to the final coat. Then she said, "Oh, I know what you're talking about now. There are a lot of buildings in the South like that."

"But it's a more recent phenomenon up North. With our harsh winters, freezing, and thawing, we've never been able to have stucco up here until maybe the last twenty years or there about. Oh, there's been stucco in the past, but it usually wouldn't last too long because of how hard and brittle it was before. It would begin to crack and have to be patched, and from then on, it looked bad. You could always see where it had been patched. This new stuff is applied over Styrofoam and allows for a certain amount of movement for different weather conditions, so it doesn't crack. Anyway, I'm sure I'm boring you with this, so tell me more about yourself."

Jackie told Ken about her likes as far as sports involvement, which seemed to perk him up because he too was athletically inclined. She decided maybe it wasn't such a good idea to tell him about herself after all, if it meant he would become more interested in her because of having more in common. Suddenly a thought occurred to her; a light was lit in her mind, and she couldn't wait for Ken to leave. She wondered why she hadn't thought about it earlier.

Chapter 11

The next morning, Jesse was bubbling over with details of babysitting for Travis and Michelle's kids. She said, "And I learned something. Do you know how to tell the difference between an Indian elephant and an African elephant?"

Rose replied, "Isn't it the size of the ears?"

"True, the African elephant does have larger ears," Jesse said, "but also the African elephant is larger than the Indian one. And do you know how I learned that? Jacob. He is so smart. How does a little boy of only two know the difference between the African and Indian elephant?"

Rose said, "He sure loves animals. Can't learn enough about them."

"Well, I, for one, am truly impressed."

Jesse had another date with James that night. He was going to take her to Champaign for dinner and a movie with another couple James was friends with. Jackie was glad another couple was going along and glad Jesse would be meeting more young ones. Hopefully, this couple would become her friends as well.

Stacy arrived two days later, Monday, from San Antonio, flying into Indianapolis at 11:30 a.m. Jackie was at the airport to meet her and drive her back to Jackie's parents' home. After Ken had left Friday night, Jackie began to hatch her plan. Stacy was her best friend in Texas. Being just one year younger than Jackie, they had met at a school PTA meeting back when both of their girls were in grade school together. They had hit it off immediately and soon were meeting twice a week to play tennis together. Jackie had convinced Stacy to join her in volunteering for different charity functions and fundraisers. They liked to think they made a difference.

Stacy had gone through a divorce three years earlier and was more than ready to find another soul mate. She had been married for twelve years when she went home early from work one day with a headache, only to find another woman in her bed. She felt she couldn't stay with her husband after that and so opted out of the marriage. Now she was ready for a permanent relationship. She had dated several men, but each time, she had decided they just didn't measure up to what she was looking for. Jackie wanted to see if she could match Stacy with Ken. Jackie had the idea that Ken might just be what Stacy was looking for—stable, mannerly, very kind, sweet, single, handsome, and, above all, looking for someone as a soul mate, not just a one-night stand. She knew if she had been looking for a husband, she would be interested in Ken herself. She thought she knew Stacy well enough to judge Ken's character as a good possibility for her.

Stacy was a beautiful woman, just thirty-seven, with a perfect shape, one that all the women they had run with had joked about being envious of. Her black, straight hair, parted on one side, was cut to chin length with no bangs and stacked slightly higher in the back at the nape. It lay perfectly in place. Her eyes were hazel, seeming to turn blue when she wore blue and green when she sported green. Her right cheek had a deep dimple that showed itself easily, even when she spoke. She turned the heads of men upon entering a room and had never lacked for a date since her divorce. However, Jackie also knew Stacy was humble about her looks. Oh, yes, they'd talked about how important looks were to get one's way in life, but she never flaunted her looks or gave an air of superiority to others because of it. Jackie was attractive but knew if placed in a beauty contest alongside Stacy, she would surely lose. Still, she was never catty like so many women were, jealous of a good-looking woman, as if they were in competition.

Jackie didn't tell Stacy what her plan was, only that she felt she really needed a close friend right then, and Stacy had dropped her work to run to Jackie's aid. She would stay for two weeks, and in that time, Jackie would do what she could to bring Ken and Stacy together. Ken would be a fool not to fall for her.

Jackie had invited Ken to stop on his way home from work Tuesday evening, saying nothing about her friend. She knew he'd be all cleaned up, as he'd been last Friday after work when he stopped to see her. She didn't know where he did that after work, didn't need to know, but was certain he would not come calling in dirty work clothing. But even if he did come dirty, he would still be a hunk who could not be ignored, and Stacy would ply her with questions after he left.

They talked all the way from Indianapolis to Stoner about what they had both been up to since they'd last seen each other. Stacy was impressed with the lush green of Illinois. Texas was in a drought, and Stacy told her Lake Travis was thirteen feet below normal and they had been put on stage one water restrictions. Needless to say, things had turned brown in Texas, and there was a burn ban in place because of fear of fires.

Stacy, of course, wanted to know if Jackie had heard from Justin since she'd left Texas. Jackie let her know that neither she nor Jesse had spoken with him, but they were both keeping busy, adjusting to the area.

Then Jackie said, "I'm thinking about not going back to Texas."

"Oh, no! Jackie, you can't mean that. Why?" Stacy had been certain that, given time, Jackie would be anxious to get back to her roots in Texas. This was not good news for her at all. This was her best friend, not one she wanted to see settle in another part of the country, far from her. When they had said their goodbyes before Jackie and Jesse left Texas, Jackie assured her the move was temporary, a couple of years or so, and Stacy had clung to that hope. She was looking at this time as a period of adjustment for Jackie, a temporary change just to get away for a while, let the wounds heal. Then she'd return to her life to pick up the pieces and move on, like she had done when she got divorced. She realized many women ran home to family, but she just knew Jackie would be back.

"Two reasons," Jackie said. "The memories. I just don't think I could ever go to the places I used to go to with Justin."

"That makes sense. And …"

"And I'm really liking it here. Jesse seems to also. I don't know. It's more than just the fact that my family is here, who I love being close to. It's the pace of life, the peace and tranquility that's here. Getting back to my roots, I guess. This move has given me the opportunity to step back, reevaluate things in my life, and decide what's really important to me. I think in Texas we were chasing the American dream. You know, the almighty dollar, the good life, as they say. The only thing is, now that I'm not there, I can see it really isn't the good life. I think we often forget what it is that is truly important.

"It seems like in Texas, we were always busy—too busy. My sister helped me to see that being too busy could have been what led to Justin and me breaking up. That perhaps we got so busy we didn't have time for each other anymore. And you must admit it really is a fast pace of life down there. You'll be surprised at how slow it is here. I've sat on the porch swing more here than I would have ever thought I could in my entire life.

"I've had time to spend with my family, and I feel I'm getting to know them all over again. No, maybe not getting to know them all over again but getting to know them better, in a way I never did before. I'm learning what's important to them, not just on the surface like it is when you visit relatives, but really what makes them tick. I can see that family is really the glue that holds it all together."

"Wow!" Stacy said. "This doesn't sound at all like the Jackie I used to know. You really have been doing some serious soul searching, haven't you?"

"Yeah, I think I have. And I really like the influence my family is having on Jesse and me.

"Jesse is getting to know her cousins for the first time in her life. She's really enjoying them and can't get enough of the little ones."

"That's great," Stacy admitted. "But I'm really going to miss you. I thought you said you were just going to come home until things were settled between you and Justin, or you got a divorce, whichever. Does this mean there's no possibility of you and Justin getting back together?"

"Does it look like one of us is even interested in trying to get back together?"

"I guess you're right." Stacy let out a sigh. "Then, if you're determined to stay here, can I come visit you once in a while?"

Jackie laughed. "What do you think? I'd be mad if you didn't."

Tuesday evening was warm and clear. After the evening meal had been cleaned up, Jackie said she wanted to show Stacy what the Midwest did for entertainment. So they each fixed a glass of iced tea and headed for the front porch. At exactly seven o'clock, Ken drove up. As he walked toward the house, Jackie stole a look at Stacy and could tell she was sizing him up.

Stacy turned to Jackie with wide eyes and arched eyebrows, as if to say, "Wow! Look at that."

Jackie said, "Hi, Ken. Come and sit with us. I'd like you to meet my best friend from Texas. Stacy, this is Ken Foltz. Ken, this is Stacy McGavin."

Ken went to Stacy, shook her hand, and said he was delighted to meet her. Jackie noticed he had examined her left hand lying in her lap, to see if she was wearing a ring. Did she detect a sparkle in his eye upon not seeing one? She thought so.

Jackie excused herself to get some iced tea and purposely took a long time returning. When she returned, Ken and Stacy were chatting animatedly, getting to know each other. Jackie was certain it had been the right thing to do, to invite Stacy for a visit. After about an hour, Ken offered to take them both out for a drink. Stacy looked at Jackie for a reaction. Jackie agreed and went in to tell her parents they were leaving for a while. She teased Don by asking if there was any certain time she was to be home.

"Very funny," he replied.

"Well, if I'm not back by midnight, you'll stay up to make certain Jesse is in on time, won't you?"

He agreed. Soon, Ken, Stacy, and Jackie were off, Ken holding the car door for each of the girls. Jackie purposely chose the back seat. Ken took them to the lounge in the local inn at the edge of the city, the only respectable place to get a drink in town. After they were seated and had ordered, Stacy asked, "So, how do you two know each other?"

Ken glanced at Jackie, who replied, "You tell her."

He told her about Jackie's mishap in the parking lot and how he'd asked for her phone number and was now spending time on her porch swing.

"Oh," Stacy replied. This told her that Ken was interested in Jackie, and she certainly didn't want to come between a budding romance.

However, Jackie set her straight by saying, "But even though he's been coming around, I told him I'm not interested in any kind of a relationship with anyone right now. And … I have a confession to make."

She set her glass down and looked at both of them with a grin on her face. "I called Stacy to come and visit me. I told her I was feeling low and needed a friend right now, but that wasn't entirely true. I wanted to … I mean … I just thought you two should meet each other. I know you're looking for someone, Ken. And I know you are too, Stacy. So I just thought I'd introduce you two and let nature take its course."

"Then you're not …" Stacy began.

"Seeing Ken? He's just been trying to help me get over Justin. We're friends, and I really like you, Ken, but only as a friend. But, pardon my saying so in front of you two, I think you two are perfect for each other. And now that you know about my plan, Ken, I'm letting you know Stacy is only going to be here for two weeks."

Ken was looking at Stacy. Stacy looked from Jackie to Ken, and when their eyes met, Stacy couldn't help but blush.

"In that case," Ken said, "maybe I'd better take some time off from work. I might have to check in in the mornings to get the guys going, but I could work it out to take several days off. What would you like to do while you're here, Stacy?"

The way he said her name made Stacy melt inside. She had immediately liked what she'd seen the minute he got out of the car at Jackie's parents'. She had sized him up as he'd walked up the walk. He was built in a natural V shape, with broad, muscular arms and chest tapering to a narrow waist and hips. He looked really good in his jeans and buttoned-up, long-sleeved shirt rolled up to just below the elbows. She liked his hair, not too long and glistening with gel so that it had the wet look. She had assumed he and Jackie were seeing each other and was baffled when Jackie got in the back seat of the car. Now it made sense.

"Oh, I don't know. I don't even know what there is to do. I'm just enjoying being able to see Jackie again."

"Now, Stacy," Jackie began. "I feel I got you up here on false pretenses, so don't feel like you've got to sit around with me. You go have fun with Ken, get to know him. And I hope you'll end up liking him as much as I do." She leaned close and whispered, "I really don't think you could do much better."

They both giggled like schoolgirls. Ken couldn't help but notice how deep Stacy's dimple was. He liked it. Matter of fact, he concluded he liked just about everything he saw. He was more than happy to get to know Stacy—in fact, eager to. He caught himself several times during the evening just staring at her. He couldn't help it. And each time she caught him staring, she'd give him a big smile. He'd always been able to carry his own in conversations with women, but tonight, for some reason, he had trouble with it, and he couldn't figure out why. But he felt happy inside just to be with the girls, listening to them talk about themselves with each other, catching up on lost time.

When he took them back to the Craig's, he asked Stacy if he could see her tomorrow, and she agreed. They agreed on a little before noon, so Ken could check in with his men first. Then he turned to Jackie and said, "Thanks, Jackie, for everything. And I mean it from the bottom of my heart."

"I know you do. I hope it works out for you two. I really do. But," she said as she gave his arm a light punch, "just you remember Stacy is my best friend, and I don't want to see her get hurt."

"Never by me. I promise."

"I believe you, Ken Foltz." She gave him a big smile and was surprised as he bent to give her a kiss on her cheek.

After he left, the girls entered the living room and dropped into chairs. Jackie was the first to speak. "So, what do you think?"

"Wow!"

"Wow?"

"Wow! What a hunk! He's just about the most gorgeous hunk I've seen in a long time. Are you sure you're not interested? I mean, if you are, I would never interfere."

"Stacy! How could you even suggest such a thing? You know I just couldn't, not yet."

"Yeah, but he might still be available for you when you are ready."

"I could never ask a man to wait for me. For how long? And what if Justin and I never get back together and I decide I don't want to get married again? No, that's not fair to any man. Besides, Ken said he's ready to get married now; he's looking."

"Well, in the car yesterday, I asked you if I could come to visit you, but I might just have to go home and pack up and move here too."

They both laughed. "If you and Ken really do become involved, that's probably right," Jackie said, "because he has his business here." Then Jackie filled her in on all that she knew about Ken.

Stacy said, "I don't see how you could resist him though, with those gorgeous eyes. Don't they just make you melt every time he looks at you? And it should be a sin for a man to have such long, curly black eyelashes."

"Yeah, I agree."

"And he is so mannerly. What man rises when a woman gets up to go to the restroom anymore? I almost dropped dead in my tracks when he did that." This brought a round of laughter before she went on. "I bet he could make one beautiful baby."

"Correction," Jackie said. "You two could make one beautiful baby together." The girls felt like they were back in high school all over again.

"Just promise me you'll tell me everything when you get back from your dates with him."

"Well, maybe not *everything*," Stacy said. "Some things are private, you know."

Chapter 12

Stacy spent Wednesday afternoon with Ken and did not arrive home till around eight o'clock. He had taken her to Champaign, where they spent the afternoon watching the Fighting Illini of the U of I practice football, sitting on the bleachers talking, getting to know each other. That evening as she and Jackie sat talking about her date, Stacy said, "I just might have to move here after all. Ken has offered me a job."

"Oh, really?" Jackie smiled but chose not to say anything about him offering her a job also and her turning it down.

"Yes, he's in need of an accountant, and who better than a CPA? So, voila, here I am, with a job and a man to boot."

"So does this mean you are serious about Ken already?"

"Are you kidding? He's just what I've been looking for. At least, he is so far. But tell me, do you know anyone who would know him that I might talk to about him? I mean, I'm not moving all the way around the world for someone who might turn out to be a real loser."

"Well, Ken did mention that he knows my grandparents, who live in his hometown. If he knows them, then I'm certain they would know him. Would you like to go see them to talk to them?"

"When can we go?"

They decided to go on Thursday, since Stacy wasn't to see Ken until Friday night.

He apologized about not being able to see her on Thursday, but he'd gotten a phone call on Wednesday while they were in Champaign, and he had to run by the job site for a few minutes. Afterward, he told her they had a problem that he would have to take care of on Thursday. They had set another date for Friday night.

Grandpa and Grandma Craig were very happy to see Jackie again and to meet Stacy. Yes, they knew Ken quite well. They had known his entire family and gave quite a glowing report about him. They knew of the construction company and that he did quality work, never taking any shortcuts for the sake of being able to pocket more for himself. His workers were happy to work for him, saying he was fair and honest and wouldn't ask them to do anything he wasn't willing to do himself. They were very happy to find out he was interested in someone after the death of his wife. They had known how hard it was on him and always felt sad for his loss. Many in the community commented that they couldn't understand how such a good person should have to go through what he did. Everyone was hoping he could find someone to love as he had his first wife.

Stacy asked, "Do you think there could be a problem, though, with people or even Ken measuring me against his first wife?"

"No," replied John. "I'm sure no one would do that. Everyone wants him to get married again. It's just so obvious how sad he is, and everyone wants him to be happy again. I know he wants to get married again."

Maude added, "If he's looking again, that's a good sign. He obviously is ready to get remarried. If I were you, I wouldn't ask him anything about his late wife."

"Why's that?" Stacy asked.

"The less you know about her, the less you'll feel you're in competition with her. Just be yourself, and let him fall in love with you for who you are, and you'll be fine. There might be some who might compare you with her, but if I were you, if anyone says anything to you about that, I'd dismiss it immediately."

"That sounds like a good piece of advice. I certainly wouldn't want to compete with someone who is dead.

"Now, can you tell me something else? Does he still live in the house where he and his first wife lived?"

"No, he sold it about a year after she died and moved into a small house. He said the memories were just too much for him to bear."

"Oh, that's great!" Stacy exclaimed. "I'd hate to think, if we were to get married, that I'd be living in a house she had decorated. If I wanted to change things, that could make him upset, maybe make him think I'm getting rid of her. He might not want those changes. This will be so much better, I believe."

"But …" Maude seemed deep in thought.

"But what?" prompted Jackie.

"Didn't he buy a little one-bedroom home over on East Madison Street, John? About two miles out of town, I think."

"I think you're right," he replied.

"One bedroom?" Stacy asked. "Sounds awfully small. But if he's got a construction company, maybe he could add a bedroom or two."

"No reason why not," he said. "That's what I did when we started having young ones. This used to be a one-bedroom house."

Stacy laughed. "I doubt at our age that we'll be having children."

Maude said, "I don't see why not. I was still having babies at your age."

"Well, I guess that's something you never know about, do you? I guess time will tell."

John changed the subject then. "Jackie, there's something Maude and I want to talk with you about as well."

"Yes," Jackie said, "the last time I was here, you mentioned something about a job you knew about."

"Yes, well, it's not a job exactly, more like a proposal. I've taken the liberty to speak to my son about this, and if you're agreeable to living here with Maude and I for the rest of our lives, we'd change our will to leave you the house and a hundred and twenty acres. What do you think about that?"

"Oh, my! Why, I don't know. I mean … this is all so sudden. I guess I will have to talk to Jesse about it since it will affect her too—where she'll live and finish out high school. I just never thought … I just don't know what to say."

"Well, your grandma and I are getting too old to keep things up around here. We really don't want to leave our farm. We'd like to spend the rest of our days here if we can. We'd be so unhappy having to adjust to living in town, or worse yet, in some high-rise apartment building for old folks. We thought, selfishly, this could work for us and also give you a good start on a new life up here in the North. And if a hundred and twenty acres isn't enough, it can be negotiated. We thought if we presented the idea to you before you get settled someplace else ... Well, you just think about our offer, and if you decide you don't want to, we'll understand."

"Oh my God! A hundred and twenty acres would be more than enough! And the house too? Wow! Thank you for giving me this opportunity. It's certainly something I can't just sneeze at, is it? I mean, I feel this just might be what I'm looking for, but I have to run it by Jesse first. It's a big responsibility. I need to give it some deep thought, see if I think I can handle it. I'll let you know soon. Oh, I do hope this can work out for both of us."

Afterward, Jackie took Stacy out to show her around the farm a little. This time, though, Jackie was looking at it through different eyes. She couldn't help but dream of how this could all be hers someday. They walked down by the pond and sat in the grass to watch a pair of ducks that had flown in and were paddling around on the water.

Stacy said, "You'd be a fool not to take them up on their offer, Jackie. You know that, don't you?"

"Yes, but I've got to convince Jesse. What if she doesn't want to live here? You know she's just now getting some friendships built up back in Stoner. She'd have to start all over again down here. I'm not sure she'd be willing to do that."

"But she only has one more year of school, and then she'd be off to college. So think about your entire future hanging in the balance here. She'll be gone, and what will you have?"

"I know. Still, I just couldn't make her any more unhappy than she already is. She's been through so much lately. Even if this is what I'd love to do, I have to put my own interests in second place to hers. I vowed to do everything in my power to make up to her for what Justin has done, and I'm going to live up to it, no matter what."

"Then I plan on doing everything in my power to help Jesse see this is the right thing for both of you." With that, she put her arm around Jackie's arm and pulled her toward the barn, saying, "Now come on. I want to see this barn."

Jackie told her the story of how their barn had burned down, how her grandpa had gotten burned trying to save their animals, and how he'd rebuilt this barn in its place. Then she said, "I just don't want to see these memories passed on to someone else when they're gone. Do you understand what I mean? They've told us all kinds of stories about their lives here, and to sell this place to someone outside of the family is like selling those memories. Does that make sense?"

"Yes, it really does. If I were in your shoes, I'd rush right back in the house, right now, and ask him where the dotted line to sign on is."

As they entered the barn, they stood in the large entry, wide enough for a tractor to drive into, while Stacy looked around her. There was a stairway leading up into the loft on the right side—an actual stairway, not just rungs nailed up on the wall as steps. There were stalls on both sides of the large entryway, the loft extending above the stalls. When she was little, her grandfather had cows and horses in the stalls on the left, she remembered, and sheep in the stalls on the right. Now, however, they were all gone. The loft was empty except for a couple of bales of straw. A couple of chickens were running around below, and a cat was snuck around a corner. Jackie couldn't help but envision more animals filling the barn, eating the grass in the pasture out behind the barn, bending down to drink from the pond. She couldn't help but plan what she would do if … Did she dare get too excited? How would Jesse react? Indeed, how would Jackie be able to keep up a place like this by herself, with no man? Would it be more than she could handle?

They exited the barn and walked down the dirt lane on the left side of the barn along the fence to the pastureland. About fifty yards back from the road and to the left of the lane was the orchard—or what was left of it. It had become neglected and overrun with tall grass. There were quite a lot of apples hanging on the trees that wouldn't be ripe for another couple of months. Jackie stood to look at all the trees. Grandpa said he had different kinds that ripened at different times—Jonathan, Granny Smiths, Red and Yellow Delicious. He had already asked if she could come and help pick when they were ready.

Yes, she wanted to live here very much. She longed for it. She stood looking at the house as they came back from the orchard. It was nice to look at, not huge, but then she didn't need a huge house. Still, it did have four bedrooms, more than enough for her, an office, and a place for Jesse to come home to visit and even bring a friend if she chose. She envisioned tearing off the front porch and adding a larger, wraparound porch with maybe a gazebo at the corner. Stacy thought it sounded like a fine idea and agreed to help if she truly did move there.

They walked to the backyard and surveyed it. Nice, big trees graced the right side, with plenty of shade around the wooden picnic table, yard furniture, and tree swing. Toward the back was an overgrown grape arbor, with a table and two chairs gracing the brick base under it. Jackie would love to light into it, trimming it back so the arbor could be useable. The left side of the house had her garden, or what used to be a garden. Now it was a weed patch, but it had the small spot where her grandma's two tomato plants were growing. She envisioned her garden in this same spot and could see the plants in her mind's eye—corn, green beans, potatoes, cucumbers, carrots, tomatoes, and much more. She could can and freeze things, just as her grandmother had done all these years. She could plant in the yard things other than garden plants, flowers, shrubs, and trees. OK, so maybe she was getting carried away. But she couldn't help herself. The possibilities were endless on what she could do with so much land.

She had to remember to ask John who rented the farmland and farmed it for him. Maybe she'd be able to draw up a contract to continue using him. And she had to find out where the boundaries of her hundred and twenty acres would be, then have it surveyed and staked. If …

Both she and Stacy were very happy on their return to Stoner, Jackie because of the possibility of inheriting her grandparents' farm and some of the land, and Stacy because of the glowing report about Ken. However, Jackie made Stacy promise not to say anything about the farm in front of Jesse before she'd had the opportunity to approach her about it first.

Friday morning was Jesse's day off from work, and Jackie said she wanted to take her out for a drive. They left shortly after ten, and after wandering around the brick streets of town for a while, they wound up at the city park. After parking, Jesse said, "OK, what's up?"

"How do you know anything's up?"

"Because you've been walking on air since getting home last night, and now you obviously want to talk to me about something."

"You know me too well. Yes, something is up, and I need to talk to you about it.

Now, before you say anything, I want you to just listen to what I've got to say. Then you think about it and tell me what you think. OK?"

"Wow! This must really be important. OK, so what is it?"

Jackie told her about the offer she'd gotten from Grandpa Craig, and Jesse said, "That's it? That's what you needed to talk to me about?"

"Well, yes," Jackie answered.

"Why do you need to talk to me about that? If they want to give you something, you certainly don't need my approval."

"But I do, sweetie. If you don't want to live—"

"Mom, I do. I would love to live on their farm. Didn't I already say I'd love to live on a farm like that?"

"But you've got to understand they'd be living with us for the rest of their lives."

"So? I love them. You know that. Grandpa is always telling me stories about what life used to be like. I love to hear them talk about the way it used to be. Go for it."

"But what about the friends you've just made here?"

"James is heading off to school in less than a month, and besides, if he wants to see me, we'd still be about the same distance from Champaign, but instead of northeast, he'd have to head southeast. He could visit whenever he wanted, same as if we were in Stoner. And as for Shelly, she's heading off to college too, and we can still be friends and get together from time to time. Besides, I just met her, so I'm not all that close to her yet. And if you really want to do this, now's the perfect time, before I start school this fall."

"Oh, Jesse, that's wonderful! I told Stacy if you didn't want to move, I wouldn't force you to."

"Mom, I'm only going to be here for one more year before college. You should do whatever you want. Think of yourself, not me."

"Oh, no, honey! You know you come first, no matter what."

"Well, I think this is something you really want, and so do I, so I say let's go for it. Living on the farm will be fun."

"In that case, let's go tell Mom and Dad."

When they broke the news to her parents, Rose said, "That's

wonderful, Jackie! I'm so happy you want the homeplace. Actually, Dad called a few days ago to talk with me about it, but he made me promise not to say anything to you about it. He had called all us kids to see how we felt about it before he said anything to you. I guess he wanted our OK since it was part of our inheritance he was giving away. But he'd gotten the blessing of all of us except me when he called. I think he left me last to call, because he knew I'd be all for it, since you're my daughter. He said the others were happy to keep the homeplace in the family and ensure they were taken care of in their later years. And there's still plenty of land for the rest of us."

"Just how big is his farm?" Jackie wanted to know.

"I think it's somewhere around twelve hundred acres. So you see, a hundred twenty acres is nothing for him to give you. Why would any of us care, unless someone wanted the home, but I'd be surprised if any of us would because we are all pretty much established where we are. The only one who's even close by is John Jr., and he's got a big, beautiful home just north of town, so he wouldn't want it. His house is almost brand-new. I think he built it a couple of years ago. So, Dad's house would be too old for him. He wouldn't even consider living in something that old."

"Why? What does he do?" Jesse asked.

"He's a lawyer with a big firm in Champaign. Makes big bucks. It would be under his dignity to live in Mom and Dad's little old farmhouse, I'm sure."

They all chuckled. Rose then added, "I'm sure he will be drawing up the papers on the deal for you."

Don then asked Jackie, "Do you think you can handle a farm by yourself, financially as well as manually?"

"I've thought about that, Dad. I plan on signing a contract with the current renter of the land. I'll keep him farming the tillable land. That should give me some income. Justin and I agreed that I would keep all the equity in our house when we sold it. I insisted because I knew it might be hard for me to get a job since I haven't worked all these years, and he certainly doesn't need it. Besides, I felt he owed me that much. So I have enough to live on till money begins coming in, and I can use that to do some work to the house I want to do.

"And I thought I could hire someone to help around the farm with the animals I want to get. I would like to raise cattle or maybe sheep. That would make more income for me. And the yard, and garden, and orchard, I figure I can keep up myself. Don't you think?"

"And just how much do you know about raising animals and gardening?"

"Well, I do know a little about gardening. Mom always had one and made us girls work in it and help put the produce up. I don't think I'll have any trouble there. But I was thinking I could get on the internet to study up on raising cattle and sheep.

"Something else I thought about was the possibility of boarding horses for people. I don't know. It's all so new, and there's so much to think about.

"And I guess Jesse and I need to move down there within the next month so we can get her registered and ready to start school there. I'll have to think about getting her a car, unless she wants to ride the bus." Jackie looked at Jesse to see the reaction.

"Not on your life," she replied.

"That's what I thought. I could ask Justin to buy you a car, I guess, but I really don't think I will. I'll see what I can find in the paper. Maybe we can pick up a good, used little something for you."

"Red, please. And sporty. I don't want any big, honking, four-door sedan."

They all laughed, and then Don said, "Sounds like you've given quite a bit of thought to this. That's good. I'm sure you'll do fine. You always had a good head on your shoulders."

Chapter 13

Jesse was very happy when she woke up Saturday morning. She lay in bed thinking about the changes in her life. She felt happy because of the prospect of getting a car, to have James, who was very interested in her, and to have a friend in Shelley, even though they had just met.

She had hit it off immediately with Shelley when she and James went out with Shelley and Brian the previous weekend. The girl, Shelley, was one year older than Jesse and had just graduated the previous year from the high school in Stoner. She was able to fill her in on everything she'd need to know, or so she said. But now everything had changed, and all the information Shelley had given her about the high school in Stoner would not be needed if Jesse was going to live in Oakley and attend that high school.

The girls found they had much in common, with the same likes in clothing, hairstyles, jewelry, and just about everything else, right down to the type of boys to date. They both were from broken homes and living with their mothers.

Shelley and Jesse had promised to get together today to do some shopping. They hoped they might be able to find some end-of-the-season clearance items in preparation for school. Shelley was entering Richland College in Champaign and would commute back and forth from her mom's home in Stoner. She told Jesse she wanted to live closer to school, but they just couldn't afford it, so she agreed to drive the hour each day back and forth to school. Jesse was looking forward to spending the day with Shelley.

She climbed out of bed, threw on a robe and slippers, and headed downstairs to scour the classifieds for a car. She sat at the table with her coffee and a bagel topped with low-fat cream cheese, the paper spread out before her. "Listen to this one," she said to her mother sitting across from her. "A 2015 Mazda Miata, mint condition, low miles, eight thousand dollars."

Jackie asked, "Red?"

"Doesn't say the color."

"Well, circle it. I can call about it. It sounds a little high for a 2015, but we could always offer less. And I can get online to check the blue book price before I call."

"If that one doesn't work out, here's another one: 1964 MG, runs good. Twenty-five thousand dollars."

Jackie laughed. "Yikes, I don't think I can afford to get a collector's car."

"I'm just kidding." Jesse put the paper down, stating it was time for her to get ready for her day with Shelley. She told Jackie she wanted to go with her if she decided to go look for a car.

"Agreed," Jackie responded.

As Jesse was leaving the kitchen, Stacy strolled in. She had gotten in later than Jesse had on her date the night before with James, and everyone was already in bed.

"Morning glory," Jackie said to her. "How was the date last night?"

"Wonderful," she said as she poured a cup of coffee and sat down opposite Jackie.

"Wonderful? That's it. Just wonderful?"

"Fantastic then."

"So, what did you do?"

"He took me to one of these places that does the dinner and a play thing. You know what I mean. Afterward, we went out for drinks and just sat and talked until they threw us out to lock up. I can't believe how fast time flies when you're having fun."

"Sounds like love is in the air," Don said, lowering the paper.

Stacy giggled. "Maybe. Anyway, I told him about your plans to move onto your grandparents' farm, and he was happy to hear that. He thinks it's a good solution for them and for you. You'll be able to have a house and land without paying for it, and they'll be taken care of. And by the way, he says if you're serious about rebuilding the front porch, he'd be glad to do it for you, no charge except for the material. What do you think of that? I think he feels indebted to you for introducing us."

"Wow! What an offer! This is just too good to be true. I can't believe it. I'd better pinch myself to see if this isn't just a dream," Jackie said.

Stacy laughed. "Well, if this is all just a dream you're having, then I'm a part of your dream, and I don't want to wake up, so if you pinch yourself, don't pinch me. I like things just as they are." They all chuckled.

"So, what's on your agenda for today?" Jackie asked.

"He's taking me fishing this afternoon. I'm not sure how I feel about that yet. I've never been fishing. But he says he has a boat down on some lake about forty-five miles from Oakley. I guess if I don't enjoy fishing, I could get a little sun while he fishes."

"That would be the Black Lake," Rose commented.

"The Black Lake," Stacy repeated. "That sounds bad. Is it named that because the water is black?"

"No, I've heard its name comes from the Black Foot Indians who once roamed this area, but that's just a rumor. Who really knows? But it's a pretty lake with lots of trees surrounding it. You'll like it for the scenery even if you don't enjoy the fishing."

Then Rose changed the subject. "Stacy, why don't you ask Ken to come tomorrow for dinner. We haven't gotten to know him at all even though he's sat on our porch quite a bit these past few weeks. I think it's time we got to know him. What do you say?"

"Thanks, Rose. I'll ask him. I'm sure he'd love it, and I know I would."

Don asked Stacy, "Would you like to take one of our cars down to Oakley to meet him? It's a shame for him to come all the way up here to get you, and then go all the way back down there, and then bring you back home tonight."

"Thanks, but I'm not sure I could find my way alone. I can do all right with a map, but then there's country roads that I just don't know if I can handle. Besides, he wants to show me his house, which he says is in the country. So, I think it would be best for him to come and get me."

Then to Jackie, she said, "I'm kind of anxious to see the house I might someday be mistress of. If it's as small as your grandparents say, I hope I'm not disappointed."

"But you already have plans for it, from what you said. So, when you see it today, just imagine it with this or that wall knocked out or moved."

"Yeah, but without his knowing what's in my mind for the future just yet."

"Right."

Don added, "You women! Conspiring like that before you've even got the ring on your finger. You ought to be ashamed of yourselves. We men don't stand a chance."

They looked at each other and smiled. "Exactly," stated Jackie.

"What's on your agenda for today, Jackie?" asked Stacy. "You can come with us if you'd like."

"Oh, no. I wouldn't dare. Besides, I have a very important date anyway."

"Really?" Stacy was intrigued. "With who?"

"More like with what? I plan on going online to learn about cattle and sheep. I figure I'd better learn as much as I can while I still have nothing but time on my hands."

"You know," said Don, "you'll have the best teacher right under your nose down there."

"Who?" Jackie asked.

"John, of course. He might be old, but his mind is still sharp. He'd be your best source of information, with years of experience under his belt."

"Oh, you're right. Why didn't I think of that? He'd probably love to tell me how to do things. As long as he didn't try to take over and end up doing too much."

"Oh, I doubt that he'd do that. He knows his limitations."

"Still, I want to have some knowledge about what I'm doing when I go down there. I'd hate for him to think I'm a total bimbo about what I'm doing. He might think he's made a big mistake."

Rose entered the conversation then. "Jackie, did Dad tell you what acreage you could have?"

"No, he said on my next visit, we'd get in the car, and he could take me around to show me all his property, and I could choose what I want.

I'm thinking I'd like to have mostly tillable land, but I'd like to have some woods too. I know he owns a lot of woods, so maybe I could get the tillable land and woods side by side, all in one lump.

"Let's see, he said the house, barn, orchard, and pasture where the pond is take up around twenty acres, so that would leave one hundred acres. If I could have about ten acres in trees, that would leave ninety for crops."

"That's not much," Don said. "You should ask him for more."

"Oh, but I couldn't. I feel like he's being more than generous as it is. I'd feel like I'm taking advantage of him."

"Suit yourself. I just don't think you'll make much money on ninety acres after paying the renter his share."

"Then I'll just have to make it up in cattle. And if I raise sheep, I can sell the wool too. Oh, I don't know. I'll figure it all out eventually."

"When you go down there next," Rose said, "you should take a hike back to the woods behind the pastureland, just to the south of it. The woods there have some really big trees—oaks, maples, some walnuts, redbud, and dogwood. And there is a little brook that meanders through it that feeds the pond in the pasture. Then directly to the south of it is farmland. So if you wanted to keep your land all together and not spread out in different places, that would be my choice. Although I don't know how much land it would be if you took both the woods and field."

"Thanks, Mom. I'll check that out. I think I remember some of that woods from when I was young and we'd go back in there to explore."

Everyone seemed to go their own way for the rest of the day. Before Rose headed out to shop for some things for tomorrow's dinner, she told Jesse to invite James as well. Don busied himself manicuring the lawn, while Stacy and Jesse left and Jackie started her research on ranching.

When Stacy returned that evening, Jackie asked, "So, what did you think of his little house?"

Stacy answered, "Well, it is quite small. It's really only three rooms and a bathroom. I would hope he would consider enlarging it, although I'd hate to ask him to. I wish there was some way to make him come up with the idea. Give me time. Somehow I bet I could get my way. It's not like he doesn't know a good contractor."

They laughed, said good night to each other, and headed off to bed.

Ken and James both showed up close to noon on Sunday. Rose, Jackie, and Stacy had busied themselves in the kitchen most of the morning, making fried chicken, mashed potatoes and gravy, a green salad, Jell-O salad, green beans and sliced tomatoes from the garden, and Rose's homemade rolls that everyone in the family loved. They would top the meal off with homemade apple and cherry pie a la mode.

Jesse and Don sat the dining room table, with Rose's fine china over her lace tablecloth over linen. Jesse was excited about the way it looked after they finished. She had never seen a finer-looking table, complete with candles at each end and cloth napkins. There would only be the seven of them, but Don had insisted they add another leaf to the table so everyone would have plenty of elbow room. The dining room was quite large, and Rose had the perfect furniture to fill it. The table could extend to seat ten, with four on each side and one at each end. More could be squeezed in if need be. With the table loaded with food and pies on the sideboard, they sat down to a scrumptious meal.

Afterward, Jackie, Rose, and Don declared they would clean up, while Stacy, Ken, Jesse, and James could relax.

"Nothing doing," declared Ken. "You girls have been working all morning on this meal, I know. I plan on helping out. I can do that much to show my appreciation for such a wonderful meal."

"Me too," each of the others added.

"Mrs. Craig," James said, "I can't remember when I've had a nicer meal. One problem, though. I feel like I'm about to explode. I ate so much."

Everyone laughed and agreed. They all pitched in to help, and before long, everything had been put away. The dishwasher was loaded and running when they left the kitchen.

Afterward, Don stretched out on the couch for his afternoon nap, while everyone else headed to the front porch, tea in hand.

"I hate to see the summer come to an end, but it won't be long before fall arrives," Rose said after everyone was seated. "It seems like every winter gets a little harder on me."

"I hate to see it come to an end too," Ken agreed, "but for a different reason. My work all but stops in winter."

"Really?" Stacy asked. "What do you do in winter then?"

"Oh, I keep my men working. We pick up work here and there, and if I don't have anything else for them to do, they can work in the shop. Winter is a good time to work over your equipment, get it ready for the next spring. You know, grease, oil, sharpen, clean. Just whatever needs to be done."

"That's nice you keep your men working even in slow times."

"They've got mouths to feed, bills to pay. They depend on me."

"Still, I think that's awfully nice of you." The more she learned about this man,

the more she came to admire him. Jackie could see how much Stacy was falling in love with Ken, and she was certain Ken felt the same way about Stacy. As she sat there contemplating everything, she couldn't help but feel this was the way life was truly to be lived, with family close and good friends to share your time with. She smiled and felt content.

"So," Ken went on, "when are you planning on moving up here, Stacy?"

"You keep asking me that."

"That's because I really want you to, and I'm sure Jackie does too. Right?"

"Absolutely!" Jackie replied. "How wonderful that would be to have my best friend living in the same town as me again."

"Well, I'm thinking about it."

"And I hope you give me an answer about it before you go back home," Ken said.

"Speaking of going back home," Jackie said, "I have a wonderful idea for next weekend I'd like to run by all of you. Stacy leaves on Monday, so I'd like to do something really nice next weekend."

Rose said, "Next weekend is the beginning of our yearly town festival, the Apple and Pork Fest."

"What's that all about?" asked Stacy.

"All the towns around have a festival of some sort every other year," Rose answered. "It's like most festivals—booths of different vendors selling their wares, lots of junk food to eat, live entertainment, rides for the kids, things like that. I usually enter the pie-baking contest. And there's other contests. Some for kids, some for adults. It's really a big deal here, and there will be a lot of people coming to town for it."

"Where would a little town like this have space for something like that?" Stacy wanted to know.

"They block off the entire downtown area. Vendors set up booths all along both sides of the street. They erect a stage at one of the main intersections for entertainment. They use the high school football field for some contest events, as well as the gymnasium for more booths. There will be parking at different locations around town and rides shuttling people to the downtown area. It's really a mad house, but I guess it brings in money for some of the local shops downtown. Don always has to rope off our yard to keep people from trampling it to death. Some of the town folks use the opportunity to have yard sales, so that pulls people out into the neighborhoods too."

Jackie asked, "Are you going to enter the pie-baking contest again this year, Mom?"

"I wouldn't pass it up for the world."

"So, what other contests do they have?" Jesse asked.

"Well, beginning Saturday morning, they always have a three-mile and a five-mile race. It costs to join the race, but the proceeds go to the schools, so it's for a good cause. Then there's the kids' races, hundred-yard dash, sack races, things like that."

Jackie said, "Bet the races are really hard with the humidity you've got up here. A three-mile race might be kind of fun to try. I might just sign up for that."

Stacy added, "Me too. Anyone else up for a little fun next weekend?"

They all agreed to sign up for the three-mile race, all except for Rose, that is. She declared that if she even tried to do something like that anymore, they'd have to call in the paramedics before she even left the starting line. This brought a round of laughter.

"Actually," Stacy said, "the festival sounds like a lot of fun. I haven't been to something like that in years. Would it be all right with you, Jackie, if we made that our big plan for next weekend?"

"That's a great idea. Probably more fun than what I had in mind anyway."

Jesse asked, "What was your idea, Mom?"

"Well, I thought we could have a card party here at Mom's."

"That would be fine with me," answered Rose, "but you might be a little worn out after the festival."

"You're probably right. Maybe we can do it another time. I suspect Stacy's going to be coming back, so we can do it on her next trip up." Jackie leaned over to give Stacy's leg a poke.

"You know it, girl," Stacy said while smiling up at Ken.

Chapter 14

July 17 dawned cooler than it had been the last couple of weeks. Jackie was grateful. This was the day of the race, and she wasn't looking forward to running in extreme heat with high humidity. Still, she opted for a bandana tied around her forehead just in case the sweat began to pour, and she encouraged Stacy and Jesse to do the same. The race was to begin at 7:00 a.m., before the heat of the day, and soon everyone had gathered on Don and Rose's front porch, ready to make the walk to the starting line at the high school. They began with stretches before the six-block walk to the school.

After the races were over, Ken and James had won in their divisions, according to their ages, but none of the three girls finished as winners. They chalked it up to the fact that they still were not acclimated to the humidity of the North. At least it was the best excuse they could come up with. However, they admitted it was fun to participate, and that was what it was really all about anyway. They all received T-shirts with the festival's name and year printed on them. Soon they were walking back toward the Righter's to shower and head back to the festival for more enjoyment.

Jackie and Rose packed up Rose's homemade pies for entering in the pie-eating contest, and when everyone was ready to head downtown once again, Jackie declared she wanted to spend the morning with her mother at the festival. They decided to meet up at the school auditorium at noon.

Jackie and Rose enjoyed the morning meandering between all the booths, examining the wares of each one after delivering the pies. That contest wouldn't be until after lunch, which afforded plenty of time for inspecting the booths. Jackie seemed certain there must be at least a hundred booths up and down each side of Main Street and splintering off on each side street, not to mention all the booths inside the school auditorium. By noon, Jackie was happy with her only purchase of a lace tablecloth for her mother, and Rose was pleasantly surprised when Jackie presented it to her. Rose had thought Jackie was buying it for herself.

At noon when they met at the school, Rose noticed James was missing and inquired about him.

"It seems the guy who was supposed to sit in the dunking booth got sick and went home. So they needed someone to fill in, and guess who volunteered?" Jesse answered.

"You mean he's in the cage over the water where people throw the ball, and if they hit the target, he gets dunked?" Ken asked.

"That's right," she said. "At least he shouldn't get too hot, right?"

Rose asked, "What's he using for a bathing suit? He surely didn't have a pair of trunks on under his clothes, did he?"

Jesse answered, "No, he's in his underwear." This brought a round of hearty laughter before she went on. "Just kidding. Actually, someone who's supposed to be the next guy in the cage loaned him a pair."

"Well, I'm feeling pretty certain I can hit a target easy enough," Ken said. "What do you say we go over and make certain he gets cooled off?"

They laughed and agreed that they all felt certain they could hit the target at least once.

So they spent the afternoon playing games, including dunking James a few times. They tasted first one thing and then another from the different food vendors, and they did a little shopping at the booths. Soon, they were all headed back to the Righter's to rest up before heading back to town for the evening entertainment.

They spent the remainder of the afternoon resting with iced tea in hand on the front porch, and by evening, they were ready to go listen to the band play and do a little dancing.

After several lively songs, the band played a slow song, and Ken turned to Stacy to ask her to dance. Jackie was so happy as she watched how easily the two of them seemed to move in rhythm together. Ken pulled Stacy tightly to him and held her there as they danced cheek to cheek. Ken was light on his feet and gently swayed his body in time with the music as they seemed to float among the other dancers. Rose leaned over to Jackie and said, "He's got good rhythm."

"My thoughts exactly," she replied.

Rose continued, "They sure seem happy together. Don't you think?"

"I believe they are. I certainly hope so."

"Of course, you didn't have anything to do with it, did you?"

Jackie acted shocked. "Me? What makes you think I had anything to do with it?"

Rose looked at her. "Like I don't know you." They both laughed.

When the next song began, it was a 1960s hit that Rose recognized. She immediately began tapping her foot with the beat. Ken picked up on it and asked her to dance.

"Oh," she protested, "you don't want to dance with me. You and Stacy look so good together. You should dance with her."

"Nothing doing," he answered as he took her hand and began leading her out onto the dance floor. She looked pleadingly at the girls, who just chuckled.

Ken surprised them all as he began to jitterbug with Rose. Rose was able to follow him easily, since that was the dance she had grown up with, even if it had been years since she'd danced the jitterbug. After the song ended and they made their way back to their group, Jackie said, "Wow, that was great. I didn't know you could dance like that, Mom."

"Neither did I," she replied.

"Did you notice the way everyone just kind of quit dancing to watch you two?" Jesse added.

"Where did you learn to dance like that?" Stacy asked Ken.

"My wife loved to dance, and she insisted we take lessons. I must admit it's been a while for me too."

"Will you teach me how to do that?" Jesse asked.

"And me too?" James wanted to know.

"Looks like we'll all sign up for lessons," Jackie agreed.

"You can roll up the rug in the living room and dance on the hardwood floor at my house," Rose offered. They all agreed it sounded like a wonderful idea.

"I've always wanted to take dance lessons, but there just never seemed to be time for it. Now maybe I'll learn some really great moves," Jackie said while demonstrating, which brought a round of laughter.

Eventually, Ken and Stacy wandered off from the others in search of the beer tent for some refreshment. James and Jesse decided to ride a few rides, and Jackie and Rose decided to head back home to be with Don, who had declared he was too tired to go out partying. Rose was happy to take home her blue ribbon from the pie contest. This made the fourth year in a row she had won, and she couldn't wait to tell Don her good news.

The next morning, Stacy told Jackie the news over their morning coffee. Ken had asked her to stay another week, and she'd accepted. They had decided they needed more time to get to know each other, that two weeks just wasn't long enough.

"I hope you don't mind," she said. "I hate to intrude on you and your parents."

"Nonsense! We'd love to have you stay. I have to admit I was really dreading you having to go back so soon once I saw how well you and Ken hit it off."

"We really have, haven't we? I just can't believe he's real. He just keeps getting better and better the more I know about him. And then just when I think he can't get any better, he does."

"I know. What a dancer! How many women last night would have loved to have had him out on that dance floor and be in his arms? Isn't it nice to know he belongs to you?"

"Well, maybe not yet, but someday, I hope."

"Oh, come on, Stacy. You know he's head over heels for you," Jackie chided. "Just look at the way he looks at you. You can tell he's so proud that you are his."

"Do you really think so?"

"I know so. Now stop worrying."

"He wants to take me up to Chicago this week for a couple of days."

"That sounds wonderful. You'll love it. There's so much to do there."

"Yeah, we thought we'd visit a couple of museums, go downtown. He says there's a little hole-in-the-wall restaurant that has the best Italian food. He claims it's the best-kept secret of the city. The owner is from Italy and opened his place twenty-five years ago down in some basement, and that's where it still is."

"Sounds romantic," Jackie assured her. "Do you think you can get another week off from work without a hassle?"

"Do you really think I care what they think about me staying another week? This is my future we're talking about here." They both laughed. "Still, I guess I should give them a call. I might not have a job much longer. If they fire me, I might have to move in with you permanently," she said with a smile as she went to the phone to call.

She came back all smiles and gave Jackie a thumbs-up about her getting another week off work. "Your future's looking brighter by the minute," Jackie said, smiling.

Ken and Stacy headed for Chicago on Tuesday, while Jackie helped Rose pick produce from her garden and put it up. They canned tomatoes on Tuesday, and on Wednesday, they worked on making ketchup and salsa. Wednesday evening, Jackie took some of it over to Sadie. When she arrived, she found Sadie and Richard parked in front of their TV sets, watching an old movie, popcorn in hand.

"Hey, Jackie, come on in," Richard said as he opened the door. Noticing a box sitting at her feet, he said, "Here, let me get that for you. Looks like some of Rose's garden."

"That's right," Jackie said. "We've been working on it for two days, and I'm so sick of tomatoes. Mom says this is the last of them, and tomorrow she's pulling out the vines. I guess I'll help her, and we'll add them to her compost pile."

"You know, she's so happy to have you back home," he said.

"So she keeps telling me. You know, it's really good to be home too. It's better than I thought it could be."

"What do you mean by that?" he asked as they walked down the hall from the front door to the kitchen.

"Oh, you know what everyone says, that once you leave home, you never feel like you fit anymore if you come back."

"And you do feel like you fit?"

"Well, it's certainly not the same as it was when I was a teenager living at home. But I'm quite comfortable at home. It feels right."

"Hey, Jackie." The voice came from behind them as Sadie entered the room. "Good to have you come by. What's that?" she said, pointing to the box Richard had set on the cabinet.

"Just garden stuff from Mom."

"She gives me so many groceries from her garden. She is quite a godsend."

"I'm sure," Jackie agreed.

"You were saying something feels right when I came in the room. What feels right?" Sadie asked.

"That I'm home. I was telling Richard that I really am happy that I came home."

Sadie put her arms around her sister and said, "And you have no idea how happy the rest of us are to have you home."

"Thanks, Sadie. You've been a real help to me. You've given me the support I've needed. The whole family has. No one is pressuring me to do anything, whether it's to get a job or call Justin to try to patch things up between us. And that's what I really needed. Just to have the time to think."

"So, what are your thoughts?" Sadie asked while Richard busied himself putting the canned goods in the pantry. "I mean, Mom says you're going to move in with Grandma and Grandpa to take care of them. Do you think you'll be happy on the farm?"

"Well," Jackie said, crossing her arms and leaning back against the cabinets, "I can't say I don't have reservations. I've never lived on a farm. I remember when we were young and would go visit them, how much fun we had there. But that's certainly not the same as living there and having to run it. I don't know a lot about farming. I feel like there's so much to learn, and it scares me to think I know so little. But I've been online trying to learn as much as I can, and Mom says to be sure to get as much information from Grandpa as I can, which I plan on doing. Still, I don't have a man to help me, and that's a concern. Even if I do know how to do something, I might not be able to do it because of lack of strength. You know, things like that."

"Well, you know you can always call on us," Richard reminded her.

"Yes, but I'm not going to be a burden to anyone. I'll get by, I'm sure. It's just all so new. Exciting but scary."

"I guess I'd feel the same way," admitted Sadie. "But if you get down there and try it out, and Grandma and Grandpa die, you could always sell the place. It's not like you'd have to stay there."

"But that would be admitting defeat, and you know I don't like to admit defeat."

"Don't I know that!" Sadie agreed. "Do you remember the time you were determined to beat me at tennis, and you wouldn't let me quit until you'd won a game?"

Jackie laughed. "And when I finally won one, you made me play one more match so you could beat me one more time. And that was after you'd already won three before I beat you once."

"Guess we're both determined to not be defeated." Sadie chuckled.

"I can vouch for that," Richard agreed.

"Hey!" Sadie chided. "You stay out of this. This is between sisters." She gave Richard's shoulder a little punch.

He stepped behind her, wrapped his arms around her, and said, "But I wouldn't want you any other way." He nibbled on her neck and then added, "Still, it would be nice to win an argument once in a while."

"Oh, please!" she protested.

Jackie laughed. "You two seem so happy together. That's the way I've always felt marriages should be."

"Oh, don't let this facade fool you. We're really as mean as junkyard dogs when no one's around," Richard said jokingly.

"I don't believe that for one minute," Jackie quipped. "So, how long have you two been married anyway?"

"Twenty-four years this fall," Sadie answered.

"Wow! Next year will be the big two five. Any plans for that?" Jackie wanted to know.

Sadie and Richard looked at each other. "We haven't even thought about it."

"Well, I think you should go on a cruise together or something."

Richard answered, "Well, we'll definitely give that some thought. That is, if Sadie would like that."

"Are you kidding?" she answered. "Who wouldn't?" Then turning to Jackie, she asked, "Would you like some popcorn? I can throw a bag in the microwave, and we have Cokes, if you'd like one."

Jackie agreed, and they spent the evening chitchatting.

Chapter 15

Jackie outlined her plan for the following weekend to everyone. She wanted to get the entire family together, her parents, grandparents, Sadie, Richard, and their two boys and their families, as well as Ken and James. She had spoken with Mac already and had invited him. On Saturday night, she hoped, if everyone didn't already have plans, they could have an old-fashioned wiener roast and hayride down at Grandma and Grandpa Craig's house. Everyone thought it was a splendid idea. Jackie told Jesse that it was traditional to have wiener roasts and hayrides in the fall when the weather began to turn cool at night, but they would just have to have theirs early this year. Mac had a tractor and flatbed wagon to use for the hayride and would make certain there was plenty of firewood split and ready for the bonfire. Jesse couldn't wait. She'd seen these kinds of things on TV, but to actually be involved would be exciting, she was sure. Stacy, too, said she'd never been to a wiener roast and thought the idea was quite nice.

"And romantic," said Ken, smiling down at her, his arm wrapped around her shoulders as they sat side by side on the swing, gently rocking back and forth.

As the evening turned to night, the lightning bugs emerged to twinkle their little lights in search of a mate. The crickets, too, seemed deafening in their quest to mate. Jackie seemed to notice how much love was all around her, and she suddenly felt sad that she wasn't included. Life had given her so much love in the past and then cruelly had taken it away. She wondered if she'd ever find it again. She doubted it—not after Justin, not after having had the very best. She knew she would never settle for less in the future, and someone like Justin came along only once in a lifetime. She sighed a heavy sigh and let her shoulders drop. Rose noticed and said, "Are you all right, Jackie?"

"Yeah," she replied. "I guess I'm just tired. This has been a big day. I think I'll turn in early, if you all don't mind." Rose excused herself also, leaving James, Jesse, Ken, and Stacy alone.

The following week seemed to speed by, Jesse working and Stacy seeing Ken every chance she got, either in the evenings if he couldn't get off work or during the day if he could. She had gotten the opportunity to show him what interested her when she challenged him to a game of tennis. She was able to beat him easily because, even though he had the strength to hit the ball, he had no control. He concluded that he needed lessons, but she insisted he only needed a little practice. He asked her if she was certain she wouldn't rather go fishing again, especially since it wasn't nearly as strenuous.

On Friday, Jackie went to the store to get food they'd need for the bonfire. On Saturday morning, Rose busied herself making potato salad, baked beans, and pies, with Jackie and Jesse lending a hand. Don had dug around in the garage for an old enamelware camping coffee pot for some hot chocolate. Sadie insisted on bringing the hot dogs, buns, relish, ketchup, mustard, and marshmallows for roasting over the fire. Mac said he would provide the drinks, ice, and sticks for roasting the hot dogs on.

When they arrived that evening, Mac had tables set up in the pastureland, with straw arranged in a circle around a large pile of logs already lit and ready to use. He had even strung a drop cord from the nearby smokehouse to provide a light for the tables. The tables were covered with red-and-white checked tablecloths, and an ice chest full of beer and soda sat at one end. He had brought out two lawn chairs for John and Maude Craig, because he was afraid they would have trouble sitting on bales of straw.

They arranged the food on the tables, John said a blessing for them, and they began putting hot dogs on sticks to roast. James stopped Jesse from putting her hot dog on her stick. "You'll be sorry if you put your hot dog on like that."

"Why?" asked Jesse, holding it in her hand.

"Because it will fall off in the fire like that. Turn the hot dog longwise instead of crosswise. Like this." He showed her how to do it and strolled over to roast his.

She came up beside him, with hers skewered properly, and asked, "Is there a right way and a wrong way to roast it?"

"Depends on the way you want your dog. If you like it burnt, put it all the way down into the fire. But if you want it cooked but not burnt, hold it up above the flames a little."

"Well, I don't like burnt food. So is this about right?" she asked as she held her stick above the flame.

He stepped over behind her, wrapped his hand around hers, and lowered her stick so that the hot dog was just above the flame. "That might be all right if you want to eat it tomorrow," he said. She turned to smile up at him, love in her eyes. He seemed embarrassed, realizing he was so close. He dropped his hand from hers, rubbing them against his jeans, and said, "Um, that's about right, like that," before he stepped back to his spot by the fire. He felt a warmth grow deep within him, and he was certain it wasn't because of the fire.

After they had eaten, Mac brought out the bag of marshmallows to roast over the fire. Stacy looked at Ken and shrugged. He got up, threaded two onto a stick, and roasted them for the two of them. Stacy declared they were the best she'd ever eaten, and he chuckled. Jesse wanted to roast her own, but after it had caught on fire, burned to a crisp, and dropped onto the ground, she gave up and asked James for help.

He laughed at her. "You don't burn it."

"No kidding," she replied. "But it just caught on fire so quickly. I didn't have time to put it out before it just dropped off. OK, smarty pants, how do you do it?"

He threaded two onto his stick, squatted onto his haunches, and held the stick high enough above the fire to melt the marshmallow— just enough to make it juicy but without burning it. When he moved his stick to Jesse, she was ready with a plate and fork. "I can't believe how you can do that," she said. "Look at this, everyone: just a tinge of brown on the outside and gooey on the inside. If he can cook this good, I think I'll have to marry him." She then popped the entire thing into her mouth. This brought a round of laughter from everyone.

All the women cleaned the table, except for Maude, who was instructed to remain seated while the others did the work. Don, Ken, John, and Mac popped another beer top and sat around the fire talking. When the women came back from the house, Rose brought the pot of chocolate to sit in the embers on the outer edge of the fire, and Jackie brought the cups.

Stacy sat down by Ken, threaded her arm around his, and hugged it to her. This was about the best night she could remember in a long time. He smiled down at her, noticing how the fire seemed to dance in her eyes. It made him feel good to have someone who wanted to be with him again, and he felt proud to have such a beautiful woman as Stacy on his arm. He hoped and prayed she would move up to Illinois from Texas. He hoped she felt the same way toward him that he felt toward her.

James and Jesse got up to move to the other side of the fire as the wind direction changed and brought the smoke, causing Jesse to choke and cough.

Rose declared the chocolate hot enough to drink. After pouring each a cup, they sat staring into the fire, which was popping and crackling as the sun began to sink lower into the sky. John regaled them with stories about the good old days when he was young and courting Maude, of raising their children on the farm with gatherings such as this one.

Ken seemed deep in thought when Stacy leaned into him and whispered, "How soon would you like me to move up here?"

"Are you serious?" he whispered, hardly believing what he was hearing.

"Well, it would take me till the end of September, I think, to give notice to my boss and train someone to fill my vacancy, pack, and get moved. That is, if you still want me to come?"

He turned to her. "You would make me the happiest man in the world if you move here. Let me come down in September to help you move."

"You would do that?"

"Are you kidding? Of course I would. I mean I will. Yes. Oh, you've got me so excited I don't know what I'm saying. But yes, I want you to come, and I want to help you."

"Then I accept your offer."

With that, Ken made the announcement to everyone that Stacy had agreed to move in September to Illinois. A burst of applause and expressions of happiness erupted from them all, especially Jackie.

Later, just before everyone left, Jackie asked John if she could speak with him a minute. After they separated from the group and began walking back toward the house, Jackie said, "Mom said I should ask you about the land just south of the pastureland."

"That's woods. Is that what you're interested in? Woods?"

"Well, she said there's a field directly beside the woods that's tillable land."

"Yes, that's right. Well, I think what you should do is come down, look the land over, and then decide."

"I'd like that. Mom said I should hike back in there to see it."

"Yes, you can. I can also take you around by car to show you all of it. Then if you want to walk any of it, that's fine. But I doubt if I can walk it with you. But when we get a surveyor to survey your acreage, he can show you the boundaries. When do you think you could come back to look things over?"

"Jesse and I talked about moving down here before she begins school this fall, so we'd need to move pretty soon. She'll need to get registered probably by the middle of August, so that doesn't leave much time."

"Well, you can move down here whenever you want. You know that. You don't have to be in any hurry to decide which land you want. You could even decide after you've moved in."

"Oh, I know. But I am kind of excited to see the land. How about I come down one day this week, just to kind of poke around?"

"That's fine. Now, about you moving in. Do you want to use your own furniture? Have us move some of our stuff out?"

"Golly! I hadn't even considered that." She contemplated this before continuing. "No, I'll tell you what. We'll move in with just our suitcases, and then we'll take our time deciding what to do about all that later, after we're here. What do you think about that?"

"That sounds great. But I just want you to know this is going to be your home too, so I want you to treat it like you would your own. If you want to change something, you go right ahead and change it. Maude and I have talked about this, and we know we'll have to be agreeable to changes, so if you want your furniture, we can get rid of some of ours."

"Thanks, Grandpa. We'll work things out. But we don't have to do it today. I just know I'm going to be very happy here."

"I certainly hope so. Your grandma is looking forward to having you and Jesse here. She's missed having young ones around ever since all the kids moved out. I just hope we won't be too much of a burden on you two."

"Don't be silly, Grandpa. I am doing this because I want to do it. I would like to think there might be someone who would look after me in my older years too. Besides, I'm building brownie points with the man upstairs," she said, smiling and pointing to the sky.

She agreed to come on Tuesday, then rounded up Jesse, James, Rose, and Don to head home. Ken said he would bring Stacy home later. Jackie said she would leave the door unlocked because she wasn't waiting up for her.

Chapter 16

Sunday morning, everyone was up for Rose's bacon, eggs, and pancake breakfast—everyone, that is, but Stacy. Jackie had heard her come in and looked at the clock on the bedside table. When she saw it was two o'clock, she knew Stacy would be sleeping in.

Finally, around ten thirty, she found her way to the kitchen in search of a strong cup of coffee.

"Did we have a late night last night?" Don asked.

All he got in return was a groan while she poured her coffee and sat down. Jackie felt sorry for her because she knew how Stacy felt about Ken and knew it would be hard to leave him. She figured they were trying to get as much time in together as they could.

"Is Ken coming up today?" Jackie asked.

Stacy nodded. "Eleven o'clock, he said."

Jackie looked at the clock. "Do you know what time it is now?"

"What time is it?"

"It's ten thirty-five."

Stacy jumped up from the table. "Oh, my God! I've got to go get ready. If he gets here before I'm ready, entertain him for me." Then she fled from the room.

"She's going to have to go home to get rested up," Don said. "She stays here much longer, and she'll be sick."

"She already is sick," Jackie said. "Love sick." They all laughed, but they could easily see it was true.

Ken arrived on time. He was given a cup of coffee and offered a seat at the kitchen table. Don asked if he could have a word privately with

Ken. After Rose, Jackie, and Jesse left the kitchen, he said, "So, Ken, what are your intentions with Stacy?"

"Well, sir, I intend to make her my wife, if she'll have me. I know we haven't known each other very long, but what I see I like. I figure once she's up here, we'll be able to get to know each other then."

"What if you come to realize she's not right for you after you've convinced her to move all the way up here? She will have given up a lot for nothing—her home, her job."

"I know. But I think I've come to know her pretty well in the past two weeks she's been here. We're not young teenagers anymore with stars in our eyes. I think we are better judges of character than we were when we were young. She told me about her asking Rose's parents about me, and she told me what they had to say. So I feel certain if she wasn't sure we'd be getting married, she wouldn't be moving here."

"Oh, I'm certain she thinks she's getting married. I just wanted to see if you were certain you are getting married too."

"Mr. Craig, let me ask you this. If you were in my shoes, would you marry her?"

"I'd be a fool not to."

"Well, then, you've answered your own question. That's exactly how I feel. I'd have asked her already, but I don't want to scare her off, moving too fast."

"Good. Now let me ask you something else," Don went on. "Are you planning on moving her into your tiny little house, because—"

"No, sir," Ken interrupted. "She doesn't know it yet, but I've been building a large log cabin on my land. When I bought that house, I bought it because it had a lot of acreage with it, woods that I'd planned to build on. I knew eventually I'd get remarried, and I wanted to build a house a woman would be proud to live in. I only live in the little house because I don't want to pay rent and have a mortgage payment too. It's only temporary, till I get the log house built. I haven't been working on the house full-time, thinking I'd get my guys to work on it this winter when there's no other work. Now, I'm thinking I need to hire some more men so I can get it done faster. But not a word to her about the house. I'd like it to be a surprise for her, after it's done, maybe even be a wedding present. I know she thinks I could enlarge the little house. She dropped plenty of hints about all the things a person could do to it."

Don smiled. "Doesn't matter about the size of the house. There will always be things women want to do to the house they live in. It could be a mansion, and I'll bet they still would want to make changes. That's just the way of a woman."

"Yes, sir. I believe that. I think that's kind of nice actually."

"So do I, but don't tell Rose that. I already have one foot in the grave as it is. No sense jumping in with both feet."

They both laughed, and then Ken said, "So, how long do you think I should wait before asking her to marry me?"

"Oh, no! You're not getting me involved with that. That is entirely up to you. If it doesn't work out, I don't want anyone pointing the finger at me, saying it was my fault.

But I do want you to know that because Stacy doesn't have any parents alive, I plan on becoming her adoptive father, so if you ever hurt her, you'll have to answer to me. However, I don't believe you will hurt her. Your feelings seem genuine enough."

"You're right about that. But I don't want to wait too long; this dating thing is killing me. When I was young and dating, it was nothing to go out till late and get up and go to school or work the next day, but I'm not sure how long I can keep this up. I'm getting too old for this."

Don laughed. "You know, Ken, I like you. You seem like a good man."

Just then, Stacy walked into the room and said, "I second that emotion."

Ken rose immediately as she crossed the room to him. He wrapped his arms around her waist and pulled her to him. "You'd better," he said with a gleam in his eye. Then turning to Don, he added, "Thanks, Mr. Craig."

"There's just one more thing," Don said. "You've got to stop with this Mr. Craig and call me Don."

"OK, Mr. Craig. Uh … Don," Ken said with a chuckle. "Well, we'd better get going if you're ready, Stacy. I have a big day planned for us."

On Monday morning, Don loaded Stacy's luggage in the car, and Jackie and Stacy headed for the airport. They met Ken at a gas station close to the interstate on their way, left their car there, and rode on to the airport with Ken. At the airport, after checking her bags in, they headed to a coffee shop in the airport since they had a little time to kill. The mood was somber, knowing that soon they would have to part, wishing they could prolong the inevitable.

After they finished their coffee, Stacy and Ken said they'd like to walk down the hallway alone if Jackie didn't mind. She said she would wait right where she was. They left the shop holding hands, and Jackie couldn't help but feel sad for them. They went to a window overlooking the loading docks and runways. Jackie could see them from where she sat as they stared out the window. Eventually, she saw Ken turn Stacy to face him, put his arms around her, and pull her close to him. Stacy laid her head on his chest, and that's when Jackie realized she was crying; she saw her shoulders shaking. September would be a long time in coming, even though it was only a little over a month away. She saw Ken lift Stacy's face to look into her eyes, then use his thumb to wipe a tear from her cheek. He traced her lips with his thumb before lowering his head to kiss her—a long, tender kiss. She couldn't take her eyes off them as they stood arms wrapped around each other, clinging to the last bit of time they had together. How her heart ached for Justin, to have someone care for her the way Ken did for Stacy, the way Justin once did for her.

Her mind began to drift to what her life was now and what it might be like in the future, on the farm, for she was determined not to dwell on what was in the past. She had to think positively, not dwell on what she no longer had but on what she would become. She thought about her family and how close she had become to them once again, happy to have rekindled the love she had almost forgotten about. She knew she had done the right thing coming home. They had not let her down, being there for her when she needed them. Family was like that, she thought—there no matter what. Blood really was thicker than water after all, as she was finding out. She felt she had let her sister down in the past, but she wouldn't do it again. She would be there for the family, as they were for her. She smiled as she thought of her family, such a wonderful family. She felt truly blessed.

However, try as she might, she couldn't help but wonder what Justin was doing at that very moment. Monday. A workday? Maybe he and what's her face were on some tropical island on vacation, basking in the sunshine on the beach, or worse, in the hotel room together. She shook her head. She had to stop dwelling on what could or could not be happening. She knew it would only bring her down, and she had been doing so well not allowing herself to drift to negative thoughts. She lifted her eyes to look at Ken and Stacy again, knowing her mood had changed because she was feeling down about seeing two people so in love, longing for it to be her.

Stacy was drying her eyes on a Kleenex, and afterward, she and Ken began to backtrack toward Jackie. She rose to meet them in the hallway. As she reached them, she laid a hand on Stacy's arm and said, "Look, Stacy, when you get back in September, I want you to know you are welcome to stay with us at Grandpa and Grandma's house. I know you'll want to find a place of your own, but you don't need to be in any hurry. Just plan on staying with us, and take your time looking for your own place."

"Thanks, Jackie, for everything. I don't think you have any idea how happy this trip has made me. I owe you so much, and here you are offering to do more for me."

"If the shoe was on the other foot, you'd do the same for me. I know it. Besides, what are friends for? I'm just glad it all seems to be working out as I had hoped." She smiled at both of them.

Stacy gave Jackie a hug and said it was time for her to get in line for screening before boarding. Jackie said, "Let me know when you're coming back so I can meet your plane, OK?"

Stacy promised to call. Jackie said goodbye, told Ken she would wait in the car, and left so they could be alone to say their goodbyes.

When Ken got to the car, he was quiet for a long time. Jackie respected it, giving him the time he needed. Eventually, he said, "I want to thank you again for introducing Stacy and me."

She responded, "Oh, that was my pleasure, believe me."

"So, how did you know we'd fall for each other?"

"I just felt so sorry for you, coming around all the time, hoping I might change my mind about dating you. It just didn't seem right to let you come around, but I didn't want to be rude and tell you I didn't want to see you. Then one night it just struck me that you two seemed perfect for each other. I knew Stacy was looking, and you were too. Well, I guess I did take a little gamble on whether Stacy would fall for you, but I felt I knew her well enough to take that gamble. And I was right.

"You, on the other hand, were a piece of cake."

"What? A piece of cake? What do you mean by that?" he complained.

"You were so ready to get married I think you'd have fallen for anything in a skirt." She glanced over at him and snickered teasingly.

"That's not true, and you know it. I'll admit I was ready—am ready—to get married. I was really getting pretty fed up with looking too, but I was *not* going to fall for just anyone. I do have my pride, you know."

"Well, anyway, I knew without a doubt you'd fall for her."

"And you were confident of that, were you?"

"Absolutely! Just look at her, Ken. My God, she could be a beauty queen, and she's got brains to boot!"

"Yeah, I know. So, let me ask you, why hasn't she married before now? She's been divorced for, what, three years. I know she's probably been pursued by dozens of men and could have had the pick of any one of them."

"You're right. She's had lots of dates with lots of guys. But in the end, each one seemed lacking in one thing or another. Stacy has her standards, and I don't think she'll settle for anything less. She and I have talked about it before, and she said one time that life is just too short to waste it on the wrong guy."

"Now that's a scary thing to know. What if I don't measure up?"

"Oh, I don't think you have much to worry about. We've talked about you, and believe me, you are exactly what she's looking for. Do you want to know what she had to say about you?"

"I'm not sure. Do you think I should know?"

"I would think you'd want to know where you stand."

"Is it something I'm going to like?"

"I think so."

"OK then."

"That first night when you came walking up to the porch, she leaned over to me and whispered, 'Wow.' Later that night, she told me she was so impressed with you. She said not only were you drop-dead gorgeous, but you had manners to boot. Of course, she thought you and I were an item, but I set her straight that you were fair game.

"Later, as she got to know you better, she bragged about your accomplishments, your reputation you've established in the community, about your eyes, your hair, your build, your sense of loyalty to your late wife, and other traits she liked, like kindness for one. She even said once that she just couldn't find anything at all to change."

Ken laughed. "Well, maybe I can keep all those ugly parts hidden till after we're married. As long as she thinks I'm just about perfect, why ruin a good thing? Right?"

"So you've pretty much decided on marrying her?"

"That's the plan, but don't tell her just yet. I want to give her time to get up here, get settled, and get to know me all over again. Then, when the time's right ..."

"That's wonderful. I'm truly happy for both of you. And to think it was because of me."

"In my book, that makes you just about on the top rung of my ladder."

Jackie laughed. "Oh, it's going to be so good to have Stacy living up here where we can pick up our friendship where we left off. I was afraid we'd only be able to see each other once in a great while after I left Texas."

"Funny how life takes all these twists and turns, isn't it?"

"It certainly is."

"Now there's something else I'm going to tell you, but you've got to promise you won't say a word to Stacy about it."

"What is it?" Jackie asked, turning toward Ken to look at him, her curiosity piqued.

"No, you've got to promise first."

"OK, I promise. Now what?"

"She thinks if we get married, we'll live in my tiny house, and I want it to stay that way. What she doesn't know is that back in the woods behind the house, hidden from the road and from my house, is a large log house I'm in the process of building."

"You're kidding!" Jackie was excited.

"I figured if I ever got married, no woman would be happy to live in that tiny little house, and I really bought the land so I could build on it. I'm just living in the little house till the big one is done. But it's not done, and I'd like to keep it a surprise so I can take her to her new home right after the wedding. That is, if I can keep it a secret from her. I'd like it to be a wedding present for her."

"Oh, Ken, that's wonderful. She will absolutely love it. I want to see it sometime after I've moved down to Oakley."

"Sure, anytime. I'm hoping to have it done sometime midwinter. Maybe, God willing, it will be ready to move in by the time we're married."

"Now, about your moving to Oakley. What are your plans?"

"I don't have a time set yet, but it will be sometime next month, probably early in the month, with school starting toward the end of the month. I'm going to Grandpa's on Tuesday to work out some details. I want to hike back into the woods to check out some of the land."

"Are you wanting to build back in the woods?"

"No, I want Grandpa's house. I love the old house. That's one of the main attractions of the farm for me. It almost makes me feel like I'm living in a different world or time period. The house just needs a few minor changes, but I don't want to update it too much because I'm afraid it will lose that charm it has."

"I know what you mean. And Stacy mentioned that you want to rip off the front porch and rebuild it. And whenever you're ready, I'd be glad to do it for you—free labor. You buy the materials."

"She mentioned that to me. That's too kind. I want you to build it, for sure. I'm not sure I could take you up on doing it for free. But it really is nice to offer."

"Look, Jackie, I feel like I owe you a lot more than a little porch. You've made me the happiest man in the world, and I plan on repaying you some way. Let me do this for you. I insist."

Jackie smiled. "Well, if you put it that way, what can I say? But it might not be just a little porch. I had planned on a wraparound with a gazebo at the corner. That might be more than you bargained for."

He looked at her with a wide grin. "I'm still getting the better deal."

She smiled back. "I agree with you."

Chapter 17

Jackie arrived back at Don and Rose's house early in the evening. Jesse came running to her the minute she entered the front door, waving a paper in her hand, saying, "I got it. I really got it."

"Got what?" Jackie asked.

"A money order from Dad for a car. See?" she answered as she held it out for her mom to see.

Jackie put her purse down and stared at the money order in disbelief. It was for ten thousand dollars. "But how …"

"I called him when we began looking for a car. He told me if I ever needed anything to just let him know. And after all, he is my dad."

"Yes, but … I guess I just didn't think he would … I mean …" Jackie couldn't seem to say what she really wanted to say, for fear of hurting Jesse's feelings.

"Mom, I still love Dad, and I know he still loves me. I just called him and told him that I was going to be living in the country and would have to ride the bus unless I got my own car and that you were looking for one for me. He said he would buy me a car, but I didn't want to say anything to you until I was certain he was serious. And now I know he really is serious. So when can we go looking?"

"Well, now that you have that much money for one, we can look on dealers' lots.

That will be better than buying from an individual anyway because you can get a warranty this way. So we can go whenever you want."

Jackie put the money order inside her purse as Jesse ran up the stairs to take a call from Shelley. Then she went into the den where her parents were and dropped into a chair.

"Tired?" Rose asked.

"Totally. I wish we lived a little closer to a large city so we didn't have to drive so far to a decent-sized airport."

Don said, "Then we'd end up living in or close to a town as busy as San Antonio. I thought you wanted to get away from that lifestyle. You said it was so fast paced."

"Oh, I know. I guess I'm going to have to give up some things in order to gain other things. I'm just tired is all."

"Was it hard for Stacy and Ken to leave each other?"

"Oh, Mom, you have no idea. And Ken says he's ready to marry her right now. I wouldn't be surprised to see a ring on her finger by the time she gets back up here, if he's planning on going down to help her move like he says."

"Want in on a little secret?" Don asked.

Jackie's ears perked up. "What?"

"He's already bought the ring."

"You've got to be kidding," Jackie said in disbelief.

Rose sat chuckling under her breath. "Well, that doesn't surprise me. It was so obvious the way he feels about her. He couldn't do enough for her when they were here,

asking if she needed him to get her a drink, rubbing her back or her feet, asking if she needed a wrap in the night air. I've never seen such doting in my life."

"He really was doting on her, wasn't he?" Jackie admitted with a little laugh. "And to think I had the first chance to get him and passed it up. Just kidding. You know I'm not interested in even looking at another man." She paused to think a few minutes. "You know, I used to think Justin was perfect and there could never be another to take his place, but in Ken's case, he just might have been an exception." With that, she excused herself to get a shower and go to bed to read before turning in. After her shower, she reached for the book she had been reading, but after rereading the same paragraph three times and still not knowing what she read, she laid the book down to think. She fell asleep thinking about Justin, only to dream about him making love to her. The dream so disturbed her she had tears streaming down her cheeks when she woke. She rolled over to look at the clock, which read 4:05 a.m.

She threw back the covers, dressed in her jogging shorts and T-shirt, and within ten minutes was pounding the pavement, determined to beat the emptiness within. She ran until she could run no longer, her legs weak and her lungs spent. Dripping with perspiration, she found herself in the city park. She dropped to a park bench, lowered her head into her hands, and wept. Could she ever be happy again?

Afterward, she came to a conclusion. She knew what she had to do. She would file for a divorce and try to move on with her life. She would be free to find someone else to fill Justin's place, even if she doubted that was truly possible. She knew she had to try.

When she returned to the house an hour later, the house was still dark and quiet,

everyone still asleep. She showered, put on makeup, dressed in clothing good for hiking, made her bed, and had coffee and breakfast started when the others began to come alive. She would leave shortly after breakfast to go to her grandparents' house.

When she reached their home, her grandpa was waiting for her, ready to take her around to survey all his property, beginning with the field behind the woods she had asked about, which he could reach by driving a mile down and turning back toward the west. Then he had her drive by other fields, dotted here and there farther from her home. He explained how he had been able to pick up a field here and there as they became available, usually at an auction, through deaths, or people giving up farming and moving away. He showed her the homes he also owned on some of these lands, which were currently rented out. He said if she was interested in one of the other homes, instead of his home, she could do that. However, she was adamant that she was only interested in his homeplace. He smiled and told her he was happy about that, happy that his home would stay within the family.

After returning to his home, she headed toward the pasture, to the woods behind. She did as he told her and followed the creek into the woods, staying close to it. Upon entering the woods a ways, she stopped to look around. When she looked upward, she was impressed at how tall the trees seemed. Some had large trunks, obviously old, while others were tall and spindly, trying to climb up to reach some of the sunlight blocked by the large trees. Smaller ones, she knew, would take over the woods after the death of the large trees. Quite a few limbs were down, caused by past storms. Leaves were thick on the ground from earlier falls and winters, making the ground almost spongy to walk on. Because the trees were so tall, there was not a lot of undergrowth, so unless a limb blocked her way, walking was very easy. With a little cleanup, the woods would be quite beautiful, and what a nice place for Travis and Drew's children to come and explore after they got older, and maybe even Jesse's future kids. That thought struck her, that she could someday be a grandmother. Could she be providing a place for wonderful memories for her future grandchildren? Yes, she decided. And she really wanted to. The woods were definitely part of what she wanted.

She continued on through the woods, encountering an occasional squirrel. The deeper into the woods she went, the darker it seemed to become, almost surreal. This was definitely a place to come to meditate, sit with nature, and let time just pass by as she communed with God. She found a log to sit on by the water and sat to rest. The water trickled as it flowed, rippling over rocks in the riverbed. She removed her shoes and socks and dangled her toes into cool water. It felt so good, relaxing, and comforting to be there. This was the way life should be lived, close to the earth, close to nature. She took the time to thank God for giving her the opportunity to own this piece of his world, and she vowed to take good care of it.

Eventually, she made her way to the other side of the woods to the tillable land her grandpa had shown her. It ran from the woods all the way to the road, which was quite wide. It was bounded on one side by the same woods she had just emerged from since it ran all the way to the road on that end of the land. The other side of the field was bounded by another road. Yes, this was the piece of land she wanted. The field seemed extremely large to her, although she wasn't quite sure how much tillable land was there versus the woods. She was not a good judge of acreage and decided to speak with her grandfather about it when she got back to the house.

She edged her way around the woods until she came to the road and then headed back to the house. After getting back to the house, John asked, "So, what do you think?"

"I think it's the most beautiful piece of land I've ever seen. And the woods are so peaceful. But tell me, how much land is in the woods and that field on the other side of it?"

"Well, it's a little over a quarter of a square mile, and add the house here, pastureland, and orchard, and you have two hundred and ten acres."

"Oh." Jackie was surprised. "I didn't know it was that much. No wonder I'm tired from the walk. Well, then, I guess I'd better rethink this. I don't really need the woods. I just thought I could sell some chopped wood to people for some income if I could find someone to cut it for me cheaply. Maybe I could just get the field on the other side and forget the woods. How much land is in the field?"

"Well, you know, this was all the original farm—the house, that woods, and that field. I'd really hate to break it up, with the woods in between eventually belonging to someone else."

Jackie could feel her shoulders drop at the thought that she'd have to forget both the woods and the field and settle for a field farther from the house.

"But," John went on, "after finding out you were possibly interested in the woods and field from Rose last weekend, Maude and I discussed it and decided it would be best to keep it all together. Therefore, I've already had Junior draw up a new will for us, leaving the house, pastureland, orchard, and the woods and the field on the other side to you. I know it's more than I told you at first, but this is what we want, to keep it all together. And I was sure you wouldn't mind if we gave you more than the original hundred. Am I right?"

Jackie couldn't respond at first. She was in shock. "But … but …" The words just wouldn't come out.

John chuckled. "No buts. It's already done. I'm just glad you liked that piece of land."

"Grandpa, this is just too much. I mean, you can't just give me that land like that. It's way too much."

"Well, it's my land. I guess I can do what I want to with it. But you're forgetting that it really isn't coming freely to you. You're going to work for it in taking care of us. You have no idea what that might entail. We might just live to be a hundred. You never know. And before we're gone, you might decide you got the raw end of the deal."

"Oh, I don't see how that's possible. Truly, I don't. This is all so unexpected." She paused before asking, "So, how much land did you say it would be?"

"Two hundred and ten acres altogether. Do you think you can handle that?"

Jackie shook her head. "Right now, I can't even handle the thought of it, let alone the actual farm. Wow! I must be dreaming, and if I am, please don't wake me up."

Jackie got back to her parents' home in the evening with the exciting news, only to find they already knew all about it. When Rose had informed her father that Jackie might be interested in the woods with the adjoining field, John said he and Maude had already decided that would be the best property to let her have, not only because it was the family's original homestead but also because it was the prettiest and, in his opinion, the best of it all. They had already decided to wait to see what Jackie wanted before telling her they intended to give her that, and they had asked Rose not to say anything to Jackie until she had the opportunity to look at the lay of the land.

Jackie said to them after they'd explained all this to her, "You know, I just can't figure out why this is all happening to me."

"Why shouldn't it be happening to you, dear?" Rose asked.

"I mean, it all sounds too good to be true. You know how they always say, if it sounds too good to be true, it probably is? Well, this sounds too good to be true, so what's the catch? Where's the fine print I'm supposed to read that spells out the flaw in it?"

Rose and Don laughed. "Maybe this is God's way of taking care of you because of the rotten deal you got in your marriage. Maybe he's making it up to you in other ways," Rose replied.

Don said, "No, I can't see God granting material wealth of any kind just because of a marriage gone sour. If that were so, we'd all be blessed every time something bad happened to us."

"Oh, you're probably right," Rose concluded. "But it is a happy thought, that she could be blessed by God in some way."

"Yeah, well, we'd all like to be blessed by him. And we should count our blessings each and every day. That's for sure. But sometimes I think things just work out for our good. It doesn't always have to be bad things that happens to us."

Jackie said, "You're right, but it sure seems like we get a lot more of the bad than the good. And I, for one, am happy to have something good happen to me for a change."

Don put his arm around his daughter's shoulders and kissed her on the forehead, saying, "Me too, honey."

On Friday, Jackie took Don and Jesse to Champaign to search for a car for Jesse. She felt she needed her father along, not only because she didn't understand automobiles other than they ran when you kept gas in them, and they needed the oil changed every two to three thousand miles, but also because she was afraid a salesman might be able to give her a rotten deal. After searching for several hours, negotiations began in earnest on a one-year-old Ford Ranger pickup.

It was amazing to see how Jesse had changed her mind from wanting a sports car to either a Jeep or a pickup. However, Jackie was adamantly against the Jeep because she'd heard of possible rollover problems, and she was secretly glad when Jesse stated she'd take a pickup because of possibly needing one on the farm later, although she decided to keep that thought to herself.

Jesse, on the other hand, was a true Texan. She settled for the Ranger but tried to persuade her mother to get her a Dodge Ram. But Jackie had reminded her that she had to buy the gas herself and might end up paying a lot for gas in a large truck. And the fact that they'd found a red Ford Ranger with low miles and a few extras that were pleasing to a teenager's eye made the decision a little easier for Jesse.

Don was able to negotiate the price for them so that with more added of Jackie's money over and above the ten thousand Justin sent Jesse, the truck would be paid for outright. Jackie felt good that Jesse would have such a new vehicle; she wouldn't worry about her on the road with a questionable older one. They would come back on Saturday to pick it up, after it was cleaned both inside and out and had the gas tank filled by the dealer, one of the things Don insisted on. He said it was the least any dealer could do if they really wanted to sell a vehicle.

They decided to order pizza to celebrate when they got home, and Jesse invited James over.

August was hot and humid, a time when things seemed to move in slow motion, when breathing in the air outside was enough to sear the lungs in one breath. The landscape was draped in a white mist, and the air was heavy with humidity even though it hadn't rained for a couple of weeks or more. People seemed to stay indoors more than they were out, trying to find a reprieve from the heat, and anyone who had the bad fortune of having a job outdoors was dripping with sweat after only fifteen or twenty minutes of being in the sun. The porch swing was abandoned, forgotten until fall when the temperatures would begin to drop in the evening.

Thankfully, when it came time for Jackie and Jesse to leave her parents' home to move to the Craig's, there was nothing to move except their clothing. Jackie made the decision that even if she wanted some of her furniture, she would forgo moving it until the the weather broke.

Jesse was registered in the high school in Oakley by mid-August. She was apprehensive to begin school in a new area but ready by the time the first day arrived.

Jackie's first task after moving was to begin spring cleaning. Thanks to air-conditioning, she could stay indoors and clean while it was hot, with the intention of moving to the outside once it began to cool down. She pulled furniture away from the walls to clean behind pieces. She stripped and waxed the kitchen floor, noting that it could use new vinyl, maybe a no-wax kind, but that would have to be put off till next spring. She was glad the windows had already been washed, but she washed the remainder of the curtains that she had not gotten to before.

One day, while resting from her work, as she sat in the living room with her grandparents, John said, "Some of the apples should be ready to be picked in September."

"Some?" Jackie asked.

"The Jonathans. Then later will be the MacKintosh, and finally the Yellow and Red Delicious."

"I didn't realize you had different kinds."

"You do know your apples, don't you?"

"Well, some. I know the Jonathans are good for baking with, and the Delicious are good for eating. Sorry, I don't know anything about the other kind. What did you call them?"

"MacKintosh. They're a good eating apple too, but I especially like them for cider. They make really good cider."

Jackie perked up. "Cider? I'd love to make homemade cider. Will you teach me how?"

They agreed to, and soon the time came for picking the apples. It wasn't as easy as she thought it would be. She had found the bushel baskets stacked neatly in one of the stalls of the barn, and after taking some of them to the orchard, she had to have Mac take a ladder back to the orchard and set it up for her because it was too long and cumbersome for her to handle. She had told him she could do the picking by herself, but after the first day, she relented and called him to see if he could help her. She had no problem picking from the ladder and even crawled up into the tree to reach apples farther away. However, she found when it came time to move the ladder, she couldn't handle it alone. She was very thankful for the extra hands, and the job was finished much faster. She hired him to come back and help her pick the others as well.

The apples were stored in the cellar in the backyard until she could make some pies to freeze, apple butter, and apple sauce. The cider was to be made with the apples with bad places on them, and she wanted to work on that first. She enjoyed making the cider, feeling like she was a real farmer at last. She was glad Jesse was in school when she made the cider, because if Jesse knew it was made from the apples with the rotten spots, she would never try some. As it was, they sat in the evening with a warm mug of cider with a cinnamon stick added to each one, enjoying the aroma and taste immensely.

Ken would be arriving in a couple of days with Stacy in tow, and Jackie wanted to get as much done as possible before her arrival. So the next two days were spent making the apple butter and apple sauce, but she didn't get around to making any pies before Stacy got there. The cans of each were labeled and stored in the pantry off the kitchen by the evening of the day Stacy arrived.

Chapter 18

When she and Ken arrived, Jackie ran out to greet her. Ken carried the luggage inside while the two chatted aimlessly about Stacy's preparations and subsequent move. Stacy couldn't praise Ken enough for his help, and Jackie couldn't help but notice the sparkle in her eyes, she was so happy. Ken seemed excited as well to have her close at last. Upon entering the house, Stacy asked, "What is that wonderful smell?"

"Apples," Jackie answered. "I've been putting up apple butter and apple sauce today, and I just finished the last batch a little while ago."

"My, aren't we just the perfect farmer now?" Stacy said.

They laughed, and Jackie said, "So far, I'm having a blast here. I hope it stays that way."

"I'm sure it will if you're truly happy here," Stacy said. "Any more apple butter or sauce to put up?"

"I don't think so, at least not with this first picking of the apples. Why?"

"Just that I'd like to help."

"How about helping make some pies then? I thought I'd make some up for the freezer and maybe give one to Mac, and I'd like to take one to each of my neighbors down the road so I can get to know them. You could help with that."

"You've got a deal. I'm a mean apple peeler from way back." They both laughed.

"What about me?" Ken asked. "Don't I get one of those pies?"

"Of course you can have one," Jackie answered. "But I figured you'd want to eat yours here where you can spend some time with certain people instead of taking one home to eat alone."

"Oh! You're right. What was I thinking?"

Ken stayed for dinner that evening, and afterward Jesse excused herself to get some homework done, and the Craigs sat down in front of the TV. Jackie, Stacy, and Ken decided to take a stroll out into the pastureland to the pond to sit on a blanket beside the water and watch the sun set. Jackie had to admit that she was happier than she'd been in a long time. She still felt she had to pinch herself to make sure it all was real.

The next day, Jackie and Stacy began pie making right after breakfast. They made twelve pies, put six in the freezer, baked six, and headed out right after lunch to deliver the baked six, first to Mac and then to the five closest neighbors, who weren't really that close at all. Not compared to life in the city anyway.

Maude had filled Jackie in on the neighbors' names and a little of their background. Most of the five were older, although none were the age of her grandparents. Most had inherited their farms from family who were now gone and who had migrated from other states generations ago in search of a better life. When they cleared the prairie grass, they found a good, rich black dirt that could grow just about anything they wanted. They had come, settled the land, made a good life for themselves, and eventually passed it on to their children. The small cemetery plots dotted around the countryside attested to it all.

They made stops at the Lake's, McClintock's, Dobbs's, and two families named Martin, a son and his parents. It took them all afternoon by the time they made the entire circuit, but Jackie was glad to get to know who her neighbors were, and she wanted them to know her in case she ever needed help of some kind. They all seemed genuinely glad to meet her and were glad to see her take over the farm for the Craigs. The little clan of neighbors seemed happy to keep the farm in the family because they thought so much of the Craigs and said they felt certain a family member would make as good a neighbor as they had been. They had been apprehensive about a stranger moving in after they were gone.

Jackie couldn't help but wonder at the difference between life in rural USA and what she had left in the big city, where people moved in and out of neighborhoods all the time, without ever getting to know anyone living around them, where it wasn't given a second thought about who your new neighbor was. The feeling of belonging, of being a part of something bigger, a plan held together by a uniting of individuals, seemed foreign to her. She liked the feeling and felt almost giddy about it. This seemed to be the way she'd seen life portrayed in movies, but she'd always thought it was just fantasy. She wondered if she would truly be able to call on her neighbors in need and if they would really be there for her. Not that she ever wanted to have to find out, but she felt drawn into the world of a close-knit community, and she knew she would do all she could to be there for any of them, should they need her help.

On their way back home, Stacy commented, "They all seem so very nice. Don't you think?"

"Yes, I really do. I think I'm going to like it here very much. And I was thinking about maybe having another wiener roast this fall, and this time we could invite all my neighbors. Good idea?"

"Absolutely. You know, in the city, I never knew most of my neighbors. I kind of like the idea of neighboring. I heard people used to do quite a bit of it in the past."

"And you know that's something I don't get. How did they have time for visiting so much? I mean, they had to work so hard on the farm."

"Yes, but they didn't have to go away each day to work. Their work was at home. So they weren't always in a rush to go here or there like we've always been. And they weren't wrapped up in all kinds of things like today. I think way back, people would be content to entertain themselves with each other, getting together, whereas today, we go to the theater, operas, rodeos, vacations, and stuff like that. We've all but forgotten what neighboring is."

"I think you're right. Maybe that's what I like so much about here. I feel like I'm going back in time. At least I'm glad to be out of the rat race of city life. I really like this slower pace of living. It seems healthier, freer, richer, and definitely more peaceful. Maybe most people are trying too hard to enrich their lives, only to find they are depleting themselves somehow, maybe in health, family togetherness, things like that."

"Sounds like you're talking about yourself and Justin."

"Maybe I am. All I know is I really like living here, like this—slow, with family and good friends near. You know, come to think of it, I believe we were trying to be rich. Materially, I mean. But all the time, what it really means to be rich has nothing to do with money or things; it has to do with family and friends, things that are the most important—or should be."

"That's certainly a profound statement. Well, I'm glad I'm one of your friends you want near."

"Oh, more than anything. I'm just so excited that you're here for good."

"I just hope I grow to love rural USA the way you do."

"Oh, you will. Trust me."

When they returned to the Craig's, there was a van out front. When they entered, John explained that he was having his furnace checked out in preparation for winter. It was something he had done every year before turning it on, a safety precaution. Jackie was glad to have him show her such things, especially since she had left the cold climate when she was too young to remember what needed to be done to get ready for winter. She asked him about other things that needed to be done. He said he would have Mac drain the oil from the lawnmower and clean and store it in the toolshed for winter. The aluminum storm windows would have to be lowered over the screens. But other than that, there wasn't much else to do, except get all the apples picked and stored.

Jackie began to make a list of these things for future reference, when John would no longer be around. She had never had to be the head of the house, chief cook and bottle washer, as well as caretaker and mother. She was glad she had always been good at multitasking and highly organized.

She also listed the name of the contractor checking out the furnace and got names and phone numbers from her grandfather on who to call should she need a plumber, electrician, mechanic, and any other name he thought she might need, including the farmer who rented the farm ground from him.

He also let her know that if she had too many apples or grapes, the local grocery store in town would purchase whatever she didn't want.

That was good to know, she concluded, because from the looks of the other apple trees, it was going to be a bumper crop this year. She loved to eat apples, plenty of them, but they would only keep for so long. She decided to put a call into the store soon to arrange a deal with them for the apples. They would be ready to begin picking within the next couple of weeks.

Then she asked if Mac would be willing to till up the garden in the fall so she would be ready to plant come spring. John gave her a list of things to amend the soil since it had been several years since a garden had been put in.

"And speaking of a mechanic," Jackie said. "What about that old car of yours out in the garage? Does it run anymore?"

"I have no idea. I used to have Mac start it up once in a while and take it for a spin, but I haven't done that in a while. The keys are in the top right-hand drawer of the desk over there if you want to give it a try."

"That would be fun. I'll do it soon."

Jesse came home from school excited to have been invited to a party of one of the girls in her English V class. She and Jesse had become friends one day during lunch, when they were discussing what they wanted to do with their futures. The girl, Carey Claypool, had said she wanted to be a writer. She wanted to write short stories for magazines or newspapers, maybe both. She was on the school newspaper staff and the yearbook staff. Jesse hadn't thought about writing, but as she listened to Carey, she became convinced that she too wanted to write. She had always enjoyed poetry and reading novels, so she decided that was what she would pursue. Afterward, each day, the girls ate lunch together, and Jesse gave Carey ideas for her next newspaper, and Carey helped Jesse write poetry.

Carey also decided to help Jesse get to know some of the other kids in the school by throwing this party—nothing fancy, just hanging out together with the girls, talking, and playing music.

Jackie phoned Carey's mother to make certain there would be proper oversight of the girls before saying yes to Jesse going. This always kind of embarrassed Jesse, but she understood why her mom felt it was necessary. It was the law within her family, and she'd grown used to it by now, but she never grew to like it. It made her feel like she was still a child, and she wished her mother would trust her to make her own decisions. However, she had to admit, after seeing the messes some of the kids she went to school with got into, she could see the wisdom of having a parent check things out first. She was proud of her mother for setting a good example in parenting, one that she hoped to be able to emulate someday.

They planned the wiener roast for the first weekend in October. Jesse made out the invitations and mailed them, and she even invited some of the girls she'd met at school. Just for fun, she mailed an invitation to Ken, even though he knew all about it.

Stacy began working for Ken soon after arriving. She came home after the first day and declared it would take her a month of Sundays to straighten out his books. "He may be a good contractor, but his balancing the ledger has a lot to be desired, although he did say Donna took care of his books for him, that he didn't have time for much paperwork other than getting up bids."

Jackie laughed. "Well, he's got you now, sweetie, and I know you'll have it all whipped up into shape before you know it. At least you can get the last part of the year organized. I just hate to think of how you're going to get through taxes with the books being in a mess for the beginning of this year till you got here."

"Don't even remind me!"

A couple of weeks after arriving, Stacy had a date with Ken on the last Saturday night of September. He took her to dinner and a concert in Champaign. Afterward, they went for drinks at a local club, then walked through a park under a full moon. Ken took Stacy's hand and pulled her down beside him on a park bench. He looked into her eyes and said, "The moon sparkles bright in your eyes."

She smiled. "And in yours as well."

"Could that be because we are both in love?"

"Probably. What do you think?"

"I think so. I really do love you, Stacy. I hope you know that."

"I do. And I love you." He bent his head to kiss her, pulling her close. His lips gently caressed hers ever so tenderly. He wanted to show her the depth of his feelings for her. His kissed caressed her neck, and she allowed her head to drop back to expose the full length of it to him.

When he found her mouth again, he was breathing heavily, the heat of the moment exciting them both.

He eventually pulled away. "There's something I have to ask you." Then he dropped to his knee in front of her and pulled out the ring box. Looking up into her sparkling eyes, he asked, "Will you marry me?"

"Oh, Ken." She took the box, opened it, and stared down at the large diamond. She was so choked up she couldn't say anything, so he began to think her answer was not going to be what he wanted to hear. The silence was like a knife in his heart.

"If it's not what you want, you can pick another one," he offered.

"No," she answered, raising her eyes to meet his. Tears glistened in her eyes in the moonlight. "It's just perfect. Yes … I mean, yes, I will marry you." Then she threw her arms around his neck and pulled him to her.

"Whew," he replied. "You had me scared there for a minute," he said as he took his place beside her on the bench again.

"I was so shocked! I just didn't expect this so soon."

"Well, I know how I feel about you. I want to spend the rest of my life with you by my side. And I was certain you felt the same toward me. So, that being the case, what should we wait for?"

"Nothing. Absolutely nothing."

"Besides, this dating stuff is really expensive, and these late nights are killing me," he said with a big grin.

She laughed and removed the ring from the box to put it on. He took it from her and slid it onto her finger. She held it up to admire it. "It's a little big, but I can get it sized," she said.

"We can do it together tomorrow if you'd like."

"That's fine. I won't ask you how much you paid for this, but it had to have set you back a lot. How many karats is it, if I might ask?"

"It's three karats, and no, I won't tell you how much it cost. But it does show you how much you mean to me. Nothing but the best for you. I want you to know that's the way it will always be. Nothing but the best."

"You know I believe you, Ken Foltz." She paused and then said, "Stacy Foltz. How does that sound? I rather like it."

"I love it," he replied. "Now what about a date for the wedding."

"Oh, my! I have no idea. This is all so fast."

"Would you consider a January wedding? I know that's probably the worst month weather wise, but I just don't think I can wait till next spring or summer."

"Wow, you really do work fast. I'll have to think about this. You know, I really don't want a big wedding, do you?"

"Not really. This is the second marriage for both of us, so what if we just do a few friends and family?"

"That sounds great. Oh, I'm just so excited. I can't wait to show it to Jackie. Come with me to her house to show her."

"Tonight?"

"Yes, please."

"That's fine." He pulled her to him and kissed her again, then said, "You've made me the happiest man alive."

"And you've made me the happiest woman alive."

Chapter 19

Stacy ran into the house just ahead of Ken after they returned to the house. She found Jackie sitting at the dining room table, trying to help Jesse with some homework. "Hi, you two," she said.

"Hey, yourself," Jackie returned. "What's up?"

"We have an announcement to make," she said, beaming at Ken.

"Don't tell me." Jackie rose from her chair and took Stacy's hand to see the ring. "Holy mackerel, look at the size of that rock." While Jesse was admiring the ring, she added, looking at Ken, "I thought you were going to give her time after getting here to fall in love with you all over again."

Stacy cried, "You already knew, and you didn't tell me?"

"And ruin all of Ken's fun? Not on your life."

"Well, I was going to wait longer than this, but well, uh … I guess I just couldn't wait any longer. Besides," he said with a grin, "she couldn't resist me. She fell in love with me the minute I got off the plane in Texas."

Stacy wrapped her arms around his waist and leaned in to him. "And how could I not?"

"So when's the happy day?" Jackie asked.

"We don't know yet," Stacy answered. "Ken wants a January wedding. What do you think?"

Jackie raised her eyebrows at Ken, as if asking, "Would your house be done by then?" What she said was "Don't get me involved in that. That's your decision. Leave me out."

Stacy said, holding her ring up to admire it, "I told him I'd have to give it some thought. We'll decide soon, together. Right?" She turned to Ken for confirmation and got a nod of his head.

Jackie hugged Stacy. "Well, I'm really happy for the both of you."

That night, Jackie cried herself to sleep. It wasn't that she was unhappy that Stacy was getting married. She was truly happy for her. But she was hurt that there was love blooming around her and leaving her out. She needed to belong to someone, to feel loved and needed, someone to share her hopes and dreams with. Maybe eventually the wounds would heal and she could move on with her life, but she knew the scar would always remain.

The next day, she rummaged through the desk drawer and found the keys to her grandfather's car, then went out to see if she could get it to run. After several attempts, she gave up. She decided to speak with Mac about the car. Perhaps he knew what to do to start it.

She decided to walk to his house to speak to him since it was such a lovely day and he only lived a quarter of a mile down the road. She found him outside loading up the garden tiller to come and till her garden spot for her.

"Oh, my! I hadn't thought you'd be able to get to it so soon. I haven't gotten anything Grandpa said to buy to put on it, and I would like you to till it under as well."

"Oh, that's all right. I can till up the sod, get rid of all the grass for now. You can get your stuff, and we'll till it under later. We'll get a good start on it now anyway. And they're calling for rain tomorrow and Monday, so it will have to wait to dry out again before I can till it after that."

"Well then. I guess we could do that. I'll try to get the cow manure and other things for later. But I came down here to ask you about Grandpa's car. Do you think you could get it running? I tried, but it just doesn't want to turn over for me."

"I'll take a look at her while I'm at the house. Want to ride back with me?"

"No, you go ahead. I'm going to jog home. I'll be there right behind you."

By the time Jackie got home, the tiller had been unloaded, and Mac was inside talking with John and Maude over a cup of coffee. It didn't take Mac any time at all to till up the garden spot, and as he got a section tilled, Jackie, with work gloves on, raked the soil, working it to remove the grass. It felt good to get into the dirt and work it. It made her excited to think that this time next year, she would have plenty of produce to show for all her planning and hard work.

Soon, Mac had it finished, and as she worked the remainder of the bed, he went in search of the car keys from John. After she finished loading the last of the grass up into a wheelbarrow to take to a compost spot in the corner of the pastureland, she put her tools away in the toolshed and headed for the house to clean up. She poured two glasses of iced tea and headed outside again to find Mac.

He had his head buried under the hood of the car when she found him. He thanked her for the tea and drank it all in one long chug, returned the glass to her, and asked if he might have another.

When she returned with the second glass for him, he had the car running, purring like a kitten.

"Wow!" she exclaimed. "You're good, Mac. Really good. I don't see how you do all the things you do."

"It was nothing your granddaddy couldn't have done if he were younger."

"I wish I'd known him then. How long have you known Grandpa?"

"Well, I've lived down the road there for going on twenty-three years now," he said as he wiped his hands on a shop rag and closed the hood of the car.

"So you've known Grandpa for a long time."

"Yep. You've got a mighty fine grandpa, if I do say so myself. He's the best of the best."

"Oh, you don't have to tell me that. I already know that."

"You know your grandpa saved my life one time."

"You're kidding. What happened?"

"It's a long story. I'll tell you about it some time, but right now, you'd better jump in old Bessie here and take her for a spin, work her kinks out a little."

"Yeah, I suppose I should." She climbed behind the steering wheel, which seemed massive, and backed out of the driveway. Soon she was clipping along the road, slowly at first but picking up speed as she felt more comfortable with the way it handled. She laughed out loud when she thought of taking Jesse for a ride when she got home from her trip to the grocery store. Now she regretted sending her and wished they could go together in her grandpa's car. But she figured it was better not to chance turning off the engine in case it wouldn't start again, so it was better that Jesse had gone in her truck. But she wondered what Jesse would think about this old car.

She felt almost like a child behind the wheel. The front bench seat seemed so large, both width wise and across the car. She glanced around the interior and marveled at the head room as well. "They sure don't make them like this anymore," she said.

She returned home, turned off the car, and started it up again, just to make sure it would start again, which it did. This was great, she decided. She would begin to drive it occasionally, just to make certain it would still run—and maybe also because she wanted to make a statement with it.

Mac had his tiller reloaded in his truck and was standing by it when she got back. Jackie went over to him and said, "How can I ever thank you enough, Mac?"

"No need to thank me; it was nothing."

"Well, it was something to me, and I thank you immensely. So," she said, changing the subject, "that's why you always do things for Grandpa, isn't it? Because he saved your life?"

"I'd do whatever he wanted anyway, even if he hadn't saved my life. But I guess you're right to a certain extent. I do feel indebted to him. Always will."

"Will you come to supper tomorrow night and tell me the story about how he saved your life then?"

"I'd love to. What time?"

They agreed on a time, and then just before saying goodbye to each other, Mac said, "It might not be a bad idea to have a mechanic check the car over some—change the oil, filters, sparkplugs, things like that—if you're planning on driving her much."

Jackie agreed to do that and headed for the house. As she entered, Maude said, "There's a phone call for you, Jackie."

"I'll take it in my bedroom," she answered as she headed down the hallway.

She was shocked when she heard the voice on the other end. "Justin," she whispered. That was all she could say.

"I'm calling to … I mean, I was wondering if we could … Look, I'm so sorry for hurting you. I wish—"

"Justin," she cut him off. She could feel her blood begin to boil, but she kept telling herself, *Stay calm. Stay calm.* "Justin, I can't talk right now." With that, she hung up the phone, whishing immediately she hadn't.

She just stood there staring down at the phone, not moving. This was all so unexpected. It infuriated her that Justin had called. She had worked so hard to try to get over the hurt, and now he called to stir up the very feelings she was trying to repress. And who did he think he was to think she would even want to speak to him after what he'd done to her? She slowly sank down in the chair and stared out the window.

What would she do if he called again? What did he want? Did he say he was sorry, or was that her imagination playing tricks on her because that was what she wanted to hear? What if he called again? Her eyes involuntarily looked back at the phone, afraid it might ring again yet willing it to. What would she do if it did? She felt so torn inside. She wanted to hate him, but she knew she loved him. She wanted to punish him, but if he were there right then, she'd want to run into his arms. She wanted to slap his face, yet she wanted to kiss him. She had never had such a turmoil churning deep within her soul. She could feel the bile rising, and she had to run to the bathroom and throw up.

She brushed her teeth, showered, and lay down on her bed in her robe, contemplating the phone call. She would have to be better prepared, should he call again. She needed to figure out just what she should say to him so she would not blurt out the wrong thing. What if he wanted to get back together, try to save their marriage? Could she forgive him? She knew her parents had worked out their problems and had a good marriage afterward. Could she and Justin do the same? Did she even want to?

And if he asked for her forgiveness and she did forgive him, would he expect her to leave Illinois and return to Texas?

She heard Jesse come home, so she slowly rose, crossed to the door, and opened it. She was just going into her bedroom. "Hey, Mom, I'm back."

"Yes, I see that." She decided not to say anything about Justin for now. "Did you see Grandpa's car out of the garage?"

"Yeah. What's that about?"

"Mac got it running for us. Want to take it for a spin?"

Her eyes widened in excitement. "Can I?"

"Sure, but I want to come along. After all, you've never driven a stick shift before. Can you wait for me to get some clothes on?"

"Yeah, great! I'll be out in the car. Hurry up."

When Jackie got outside, Jesse was already behind the wheel. "Where's the radio?" she asked.

"I suppose you can't drive a car that doesn't have a radio," Jackie said, tossing the keys to her.

"Well, I didn't say that. But it sure would be nice if it had one. Talk about boring without it."

"There really was life before radios, you know. I know that's hard to fathom, but trust me on this one."

"Funny." Jesse gave her mother a mock smile and started the car.

Jackie explained how to drive a shift, with Jesse nodding the entire time like she understood completely. She shifted into first and promptly took her foot off the clutch, causing the car to lurch forward and die. Jackie went over everything a second time. Jesse said, "Well, that's what I thought I did." But in starting the car again and forgetting to push in on the clutch, the car lurched forward again.

Jesse hit the steering wheel with her fist in anger while Jackie laughed.

"Want to switch places with me?" Jackie offered.

"Wait. Let me try one more time. I push in on the clutch," she said as she did so. "Then I start the car. OK, so far, so good. Now, how do I know how much gas to give it so it won't jump again?"

"Well, that's not something I can really tell you. You'll just have to practice till you feel comfortable with it. You just learn it as you go. Just give it a try, but ease off the clutch slower this time."

Jesse revved up the engine much more than she needed to but didn't release the clutch at all.

"OK, that was nice," Jackie said. "Now do you think you could ease off the clutch a little so we might actually move?"

Jesse broke out in a laugh. "Stop! I can't do this with you over there making fun of me." Then trying to get herself under control, she said, "OK, here goes."

This time, the car only jumped slightly, then a second time, and then they were moving down the road. "I did it!" she exclaimed. "I really did it!"

"You see? All it takes is a little practice."

She did just fine until she had to stop. She forgot to push in the clutch as she put on the brake, and Jackie had to yell at her to do it. She finally got that down but killed the car after another lurch when she tried to start up again. This time she got out, changed places with Jackie, and refused to drive back home.

"All you need is practice. It's just like when you took driver's ed in school. You had to start sometime behind the wheel. Keep trying, and soon you'll be a pro just like me."

"Yeah, right."

Chapter 20

On Monday, Jackie purchased the cow manure she needed for her garden, along with the things she needed for dinner in the evening. She had also purchased stakes with the names of plants on them to put at the end of each row after planting next spring, along with tomato cages and string and stakes to tie up the pole beans. It felt good to know she was ready to begin raising her food come spring.

After unloading the groceries and putting them away, she headed out to spread the manure over the soil in the garden. Later, she worked on baking blackberry pie for dinner. They had given Mac blackberry jelly, and he'd commented that he loved blackberries, so she was certain the pie would be a success. She prepared lasagna ahead of time so all she had to do was pop it into the oven, make the salad, and toast the garlic Texas toast. After she was finished, she poured a glass of iced tea and went to sit with her grandparents for a while.

Maude was stitching her quilt top and accepted help when Jackie offered. Maude was insistent that each stitch was to be done by hand— "the real way to make a quilt," as she put it. Jackie knew her stitches weren't as even as Maude's, but if Maude didn't mind allowing her to help out, it would be good practice. John sat working a crossword puzzle.

Jackie looked up from her sewing and said to John, "Mac said he'll tell me tonight about how you saved his life."

John lowered his paper. "He did, did he?"

"Yes, and don't you tell me anything about it. I want to hear it from him."

"That's fine with me. I'm just surprised he wants to tell you. You must be very special. That's not something he will talk about usually."

"Why won't he talk about it? I'd think he'd be happy to tell people how you saved his life. You're the one I would think who wouldn't want to tell people about it, for fear it would look like you were tooting your own horn."

"I'm not going to say any more than that. It's up to him to tell you how much he wants you to know."

"Well, now you've got my curiosity up."

"Like you said, he's going to tell you, so let him tell it. But you're not having anyone else in for dinner, are you? Because if you are, I can guarantee you he won't tell you about it."

"No, no one. Ken's taking Stacy out somewhere tonight, so it should be just us and Mac. But this is all so mysterious."

"You'll understand after you hear what he has to say."

It began to sprinkle outside, and before long, it was pouring. Jackie worried about Jesse driving home from school but knew she was a good driver. She'd learned to drive in San Antonio, where the traffic was horrific, so Jackie was certain if she could drive there, she could drive anywhere. As it was, the rain had stopped by the time Jesse got out of school, so she walked in the door only fifteen minutes later than usual.

"Something smells heavenly," she said as she threw her books and jacket down in a nearby chair.

"Hi, honey," Jackie said. "It's a blackberry pie for supper. It's a good thing you got some ice cream yesterday. We'll have it too."

"What's the special occasion?"

"No special occasion. Mac is just coming for supper, and I know he doesn't have anyone to bake pies for him."

"That's nice. Any tea made?" she asked as she headed toward the kitchen.

"There's a little left. Why don't you finish it up and make another pitcher for tonight? Do you have much homework?"

"Just a test to study for, but I can do it after dinner. I don't think it will be a hard one."

"Good. Then you can make the salad for dinner and turn on the oven to three fifty. I need to throw the lasagna in soon."

Mac arrived at 5:30, punctual as always. Everyone was in agreement that Jackie made the best lasagna east of the Mississippi. She took the compliment graciously, then turned the conversation to Mac.

"Mac, you said you'd tell me how Grandpa saved your life."

"Yes, I did, didn't I?" He chewed his bottom lip, contemplating where to begin. He took a deep breath and said, "Well, like I told you, we moved here about twenty-three years ago. Janice, my wife, was pregnant at the time. We'd been living in town in an apartment up until then, but with a baby on the way, we wanted a place to raise him. She didn't think an apartment was a good place—said he needed a yard to run and play in. So we began looking around for a place, and eventually we found this place here in the country."

Jackie couldn't imagine what any of this had to do with John saving Mac's life, but she held her questions as he went on.

"Anyway, we bought the place and moved in when Janice was in her eighth month of pregnancy. We'd met John and Maude and the other neighbors around and liked them a lot." He paused to gather his thoughts before continuing. "We were so happy here in the country. Then one day in December, she and I went to town for some things. The roads were slick after a rain because the temperature had dropped drastically."

Jackie's stomach began to churn. She was fearful of where this was going and dreaded ever asking Mac about it. Suddenly she knew why her grandfather had said Mac never wanted to talk about it. She looked at John, who was watching for her reaction.

"Mac," she interrupted. "You don't have to tell me this if you don't want to."

He turned to look at her, his expression full of pain. "It's all right. It was a long time ago, twenty-three years this December to be exact." He took a deep breath and continued, "So, here we were coming home from town on icy roads, roads we weren't that familiar with yet. Somehow, I lost control of the car on a curve. The next thing I know, we're spinning round and round in the road. Then we hit a guard rail on the curve and flipped. I don't know how many times we rolled—one or two maybe. When I came to, John was busting out my side window of the car. He dragged me from the car and then Janice. She was unconscious.

"He put us in his car and drove us all the way to the hospital, an hour away in Champaign. They took the baby, but Janice didn't live. So there you have it."

"Oh, Mac, I'm so sorry. I had no idea it had anything to do with your wife's death. I would never have asked if …"

"That's OK. If we're to be neighbors, I guess you need to know a little something about us. And like I said, it was a long time ago."

"Did the baby … I mean, what happened?"

"He lived, thankfully. I guess because she was close to full-term. He had to stay in the hospital for a couple of weeks though. I named him Jacob, after my father. He's off to college now, out in Colorado. Gonna be a chiropractor. I'm mighty proud of him."

Jackie smiled. "I bet you are. So you raised him alone?"

"Hell, no! Pardon my language. That just slipped out. I couldn't raise him alone. I had to work. My mom came and stayed with me for a couple of months to help me get back on my feet. I was pretty banged up myself from the wreck. I had a broken leg, a broken rib, and a broken jaw. But once I got back on my feet, she left, and Maude here stepped in. She pretty much raised Jake for me, I'd say, and I'm mighty beholden to her for all she's done for me. She did a right good job too. And I'm mighty beholden to John too, because if he hadn't come along and helped us, I might not have lived either, because my rib had punctured my lung, and I could have died if I hadn't gotten to the hospital as quickly as I did. So they tell me."

Jackie smiled at John. "I'm glad you were able to save him and his son, Grandpa.

It's too bad about Janice though."

Mac said, "Everyone around tried to fill the void for me, especially for Jake. We were always invited to someone's house for a meal, and quite often, Jake would spend the night. But when he needed loving, he would run to Maude. I really think she became his mom."

"I can see Grandma doing that." Jackie winked at Maude. "Grandma has always had a soft spot in her heart for little ones, as I recall growing up."

"And you should have seen him," Maude said. "A prettier boy I've never laid eyes on. He has the most beautiful blue eyes and the longest lashes I've ever seen on anyone. And he's got curly black hair. He's really quite handsome."

"And he's twenty-three?" asked Jesse.

"He will be this December 16," answered Mac.

"So when do I get to meet him?" she asked.

Everyone laughed. "Oh, I see what you've got up your sleeve," Jackie said.

"Well, anyone who sounds that good-looking is someone worth checking into, wouldn't you say?"

"Just remember you've got college ahead of you, young lady," Jackie reminded her.

"So? Who says I'm ready for marriage right now anyway? No harm in looking, is there?"

"You'll get to meet him this Christmas. He'll be home for the holidays," Mac said, "and I know he'll want to meet you."

"What about James?" Jackie asked.

"Who says there's only one fish in the sea?" Jesse asked, and everyone laughed.

"Oh, to be young again," Mac said.

"Is that why you never got married after that? Because of your son?" Jackie asked.

"Well, there just wasn't any time to think about myself. My main concern was for my son. And after being away from him all day working, I just couldn't leave him in the evenings to hunt for a new wife. I did think about it, of course, but I was afraid a new wife wouldn't love him the way he'd need to be loved. So in the end, I decided to just leave well enough alone. Maude was more than enough mom for him anyway."

"Thanks, Mac," Maude said. "I wouldn't have wanted it any other way."

"And when I think of all the times your grandma sat up with Jake nearly all night because of some sickness or other and watched him after school every day till I got home ... Well, I guess you can see why I like to do whatever I can for them now."

"And that's the way it should be, right? Neighbors who are there for each other whenever they need?" Jackie asked.

"That's right," Maude said. "Lord, I don't know where we would be today if we didn't have Mac." Then turning to Mac, she asked, "Do you remember, Mac, the time we came home from the doctor's and had locked ourselves out of the house?"

John, Maude, and Mac laughed. "I suppose we could have gotten a ladder and crawled through that window like you did, but I can't see John or me at eighty trying to crawl through a window.

"Then there's the time John twisted his ankle on the steps out front, and I had to call you to come and help him up. Then you came and fed the chickens every day and tended the garden for us."

"That's the year I decided to quit putting in a garden," John said.

The remainder of the evening was spent reminiscing. Jackie enjoyed listening to all their stories. Jesse, though, had to get her homework done and had to excuse herself shortly after eating. Jackie teasingly accused her of making up the homework so she could get out of doing the dishes.

"I'll trade places with you then," Jesse offered. "I'll do the dishes if you'll take my test for me tomorrow."

Jackie threw her napkin at Jesse and said, "Go on. Get out of here."

Chapter 21

Soon it was time for the wiener roast, and Mac once again set bales of straw around the bonfire for everyone to set on, then rigged his flatbed trailer with straw for the hayride. He knew all the off-road farmer's access dirt roads and offered to drive the tractor. All the neighbors, Jesse's friends from school, and Ken came and had a wonderful time. The neighbors said they were glad to get better acquainted with their new neighbors. They already knew Ken but said it was really nice to be able to congratulate him on his upcoming wedding, especially to someone as nice looking as Stacy. It was so obvious that Ken was proud to say she belonged to him.

John and Maude decided to go inside when they all climbed on the wagon after dark for the hayride. Someone decided to tell a scary story. Then others joined in with more, until finally one of the women rebelled and asked if they could sing songs instead. By the time they were back to the bonfire, they were belting out "Home on the Range" at the top of their voices.

Everyone eventually headed for home, happy and firmly determined to do things like that more often.

As they were saying goodbye to the last couple, John came to the door and called out to Jackie that she had a phone call. Her stomach did a flip as she turned to go to the house.

"Hello," she answered tentatively.

"Jackie," Justin said, almost pleadingly.

She was prepared this time. "What do you want, Justin?"

"I want to talk with you. I want to apologize to you. I want to come back to you."

Jackie was fuming. "Just like that?" she stormed. "You apologize, and I'm supposed to say, 'I'm sorry. Come on home'?"

"No, I would never expect that. But won't you please just talk to me?"

"And you think you can just call me up, and we can resolve all our differences over the phone?"

"Well, we have to start somewhere."

"No! I'm not even considering anything over a phone conversation. You can't expect to work out any problem by phone."

"Then come home. I want you back. Please," he begged.

"I'm not leaving Illinois, Justin. Jesse is in school, and I won't take her out. If you want to talk to me, I guess you'll have to come up here." She regretted having said it the minute the words slipped from her tongue.

"Will you at least talk to me if I come up?"

There was a long pause as Jackie mulled this over in her mind. "No promises, Justin. I just can't."

"I guess I deserved that. Look, I'm coming up just as soon as I can get my schedule rearranged. Should I call you when I get there?"

"You can do whatever …" she started but caught herself before saying what she really wanted to say. "Whatever. Goodbye." She returned the phone to the cradle.

When she turned around, there stood Jesse. "Mom? Was that dad?"

"Yes," Jackie answered. "He's coming to Illinois."

"Good. Now maybe you two can get back together," Jesse said hopefully.

"Jesse, if you heard what I said to Justin, you know I told him, 'No promises.' I wouldn't get my hopes up if I were you."

"But I know Dad still loves you, and I know you love him. So what's wrong with giving it a try again?"

"It's not that easy, honey. I know he loved me once, but if you truly love someone, you don't hurt them like he hurt me. That's not love. So I wouldn't say he loves me, not anymore." Jackie turned to go to the kitchen to put things away.

"But he told me how much he loves you and how sorry he is that he did what he did."

Jackie twirled around. "When did he tell you that?"

"When I talked to him on the phone. We've been talking to each other every week since we left Texas."

"You've what?" Jackie couldn't believe what she was hearing. "Why didn't you tell me you've been in touch with him all along? I thought the only time you'd spoken with him was when you called him about your truck."

"Well, I didn't tell you about it because I thought you'd get mad at me because I still wanted a relationship with him, even if you didn't. So we would call each other on our cell phones every Friday night, just to check in with each other to see how the other one was doing."

"Oh, Jesse." Jackie crossed the room and gave Jesse a hug. "I never meant for you to give up your father just because he and I were no longer together. He's your father and will always be your father. Actually, knowing about you two staying in touch with each other makes me feel much better about things."

"Why's that?" Jesse asked.

"Because it's one thing for a marriage to go sour and break up, but I thought he was turning his back on you as well. I had no idea you two were staying in touch. I thought he had turned his back on both of us. I'm so glad to hear he's stayed in touch with you."

"Do you want to know what he said?"

"I'm not sure I should know. What you two talk about is between you two."

"But, Mom, he said he knows how stupid he's been. He's really hurting inside."

"He said that?"

"No, but I can tell. He tried not to let me know, but I could tell he was having a hard time trying not to cry the last time we talked to each other."

Jackie mulled over this new information. It made her feel good to know Justin had continued trying to take care of his daughter, even though it was from such a long distance. The pain of knowing he had turned his back on his daughter had hurt Jackie even more than what he'd done to her. She should have known he could never shirk his responsibility to Jesse. Hadn't he always been the perfect father?

"So, will you at least try to forgive him? For me? Please?" Jesse said.

"I love you, Jesse. You know that." Jackie gave her another hug. "I've got a lot to think about. But I still can't promise anything. I hope you understand. There's just so much to think about and talk about and issues to work through."

Jesse returned her mother's hug and said, "I know, but I also know you still love Dad. I guess I'm just so anxious for you two to patch things up. It seems to me like if two people love each other, they should be able to work through their problems."

"I love you, Jess."

"I love you too, Mom."

"I wish life could be that easy, especially for your happiness."

After getting into bed, sleep did not come for quite some time for Jackie. She did still love Justin, yet she knew if she just allowed him back into her life without a resolution of some kind, there would be nothing to stop him from doing the same thing again in the future. What guarantee would she have? How could she make sure he understood that she could never forgive him again for doing the same thing? And thoughts of giving up her opportunity to gain a farm and a peaceful life she had grown to love were overwhelming.

As she lay in the dark, thoughts whirled inside her mind, sad thoughts of leaving her family, of leaving the farm and returning to the city life of San Antonio. She couldn't stop the tear that escaped the corner of her eye and trickled down her cheek and onto her pillow. How could she just give it all up so quickly after finding what she came to realize she had always missed in her life? And if she returned to Texas, she would be leaving behind her best friend in Illinois as well.

But utmost in her mind was what would be best for Jesse. Where would she be happiest—in Texas or here? Did it even matter to her? She hadn't asked her where she preferred to live or go to college.

When she woke the next morning, her head was throbbing with pain. She had slept fitfully, waking every couple of hours and mulling things over in her mind some more. She dragged herself from the bed in search of headache medicine and coffee.

The day didn't go any better. She wasn't able to accomplish anything, and by afternoon, she gave up trying and headed for her bedroom for a much-needed nap. When she awoke, she felt much better and was ready to greet Jesse upon her return from a school football game with a couple of her girlfriends in tow. She even felt good enough to take them out for pizza that evening.

That night, she fell into bed ready to sleep, even though her mind was still troubled. The next day, after Jesse left for school, she told her grandparents she was going to visit her parents for the day and headed to their home.

They were busy as usual when she arrived. Her mother was covering some of her plants for the winter with straw, while her father was removing the old wooden screens and replacing them with storm windows. She had coffee ready for them when they needed a break.

While they sat in the kitchen, Jackie breached the subject she had come to talk to them about. "Mom, Dad, I have something to ask you two about. I need to know about something, and I don't know any place else to turn."

"What is it, dear?" Rose said as she took Jackie's hand in her own.

"Well, Grandma and Grandpa have told me about the trouble you two had years ago and how you almost broke up."

Rose and Don looked at each other.

"Now don't get mad at them for telling me. They only told me because they wanted me to see that it is possible to mess up a marriage and still be able to have things work out and be happy."

Rose replied, "We've talked about that ourselves, since this has all come up between you and Justin. We didn't know if we should tell you about our problems. We didn't want you to feel differently toward your father. So we just decided to wait and see what happened before we did anything."

"Well, I can't say it wasn't a shock. It took quite a lot of thinking about things before I could come to grips with it. You two have always seemed so happy with each other that I just couldn't believe what they were saying at first. But now … well, I wasn't going to say anything to either of you about my knowing because I figured if you'd wanted me to know, you would have said something. And when you didn't, I figured you weren't going to tell me. But Justin has called me, and he wants to come here to try to work things out between us, and that's why I'm here."

"But that's wonderful," Rose said excitedly. "I've been praying that you two could work things out. You are happy about that, aren't you?"

"To tell you the truth, I'm not sure how I feel about it. I still love him, and I guess I always will. But I'm scared to death. I need to know how you two were able to work through it all."

Rose looked at Don before continuing. "I know exactly how you're feeling, honey. You love him, but you hate him at the same time."

"Exactly!" Jackie exclaimed.

"When I left Don, I had decided our marriage was over, that I could never forgive him. I was so determined to get a divorce. I just knew there would be no way to ever mend things between us. He came to talk to me, and I refused to talk." She let out a little chuckle before continuing. "I even locked myself in my bedroom so he couldn't get to me to persuade me to go back to him. My mind was made up."

"But Grandma talked you into talking with him. Right?"

"She knocked on my door, and we talked. She helped me to see that communication was important, even if we did get a divorce, because there would be things that would have to be worked out between us no matter if we stayed together or not." Then with a smile on her face as she looked at Don, she said, "And it didn't hurt to tell me that Don had said he wasn't going to leave till I talked with him, no matter how long it took before I came out of the bedroom."

"But I need to know how you were able to still have a happy marriage for so many years afterward. At least Sadie and I always thought you had a happy marriage."

"Yes, I'd say we have. You see…"

Don interrupted Rose then. "You see, Jackie, every marriage will have its ups and downs. I can't excuse what I did to your mother. I know I hurt her deeply. I've regretted what I did, and I will regret it to my dying day. I can't undo the past; what is done is done. Lord knows I've apologized to her enough down through the years, and I never forget what I've got in a wonderful wife. I don't think I will ever be able to make it up to her.

"There's something you need to understand about men—all men. I think you women think men are the stronger sex, but I've come to the realization that women are the stronger of the two."

"How's that?" Jackie asked.

"Men can be swayed so easily sometimes if they let their guard down. If a pretty woman just walks by, it's everything a man can do not to turn and look at her. And when men are constantly around a pretty woman on a regular basis, it almost becomes too overpowering not to act on the instinct to go after her. I'm not saying that's right, but it's true. And the younger the man, the harder it is to control those impulses."

Jackie knit her brow together and said, "Well, Justin certainly isn't like some young boy who can't control his runaway hormones."

"No," Don continued, "but if your relationship had grown stagnant, maybe he had needs that weren't being met. I'm not saying that was the case. Only you can answer that. What I'm trying to tell you is that men are attracted to good-looking women, *all* good-looking women. And sometimes it gets them into trouble. But that doesn't mean he doesn't love you any less. It only means he messed up royally. But now he's come to his senses, and he knows how badly he messed up."

"So, Mom, what made you change your mind about getting a divorce?"

"Don did. We talked and talked that night. Don admitted he was wrong and vowed to never do it again. He was so repentant that he convinced me to believe in him one more time. However, I did tell him that if it ever happened again, that would be it. Our marriage would be over—no ifs, ands, or buts, that he couldn't even ask for my forgiveness a second time. And I must admit it took years before I felt I could really trust him. I guess once that trust is broken, it's hard to get it back. But we both agreed that night after we decided to try again that neither of us would ever bring it up to the other one again. However, your father couldn't live by that because he felt he had to apologize about five million times, and he's tried to do things to show how much he loves me over the years. Maybe because of what we've been through, it made us work all the harder to have our marriage work and made us happier in the long run."

"One thing about it," Dan said, "is we've come to know without a doubt that the way to be happily married is to give of yourself to your mate for what makes *them* happy, not for what makes *you* happy. I feel like I've spent most of my marriage trying to make up for that one mistake I made, but I've been the happiest man alive since then, and it's all because of Rose and her forgiving attitude about it."

"So, you think Justin and I could make it work again?"

"That's between you two. All we're saying is don't be too quick to give up. What you two had at one time was real. Everyone around you could see that. If you two can work through it and forgive, I don't see why you couldn't still find happiness," Rose said. "But as I said, that's between you two. If you should decide to forgive him, then you must—and I mean *must*—forget it. You can't bring it up and throw it in his face every time you get into an argument about something. And you will have a hard time worrying about whether he's being faithful to you or not, but given time, even that can change. Even though I always wondered what Don was doing or who he was with, I never let on to him that I didn't trust him. That would have been a slow, festering wound that would have eventually erupted into a battle we might not have recovered from."

Jackie looked down at her hands, her head spinning with all they had told her. Don ended the discussion by saying, "You don't have to make a decision today about anything. You haven't even spoken to Justin yet. But when you do, I'm sure he'll try to help you understand what drove him to do what he did. Just try to see things from his point of view. And I don't mean for you to condone what he did at all. But try to put yourself in his shoes, feel what he was feeling when he erred. Maybe that will help you to understand him a little better. And just remember, it takes two to make a good marriage, and it takes two to make a bad marriage. So if you two want to stay together, you will both have to be willing to work at it, always doing what is best for the other one. And the reward for doing so will be happiness. Right, Rose?"

"I couldn't have said it better if I'd tried," she agreed.

Jackie took a deep breath. "Thanks, both of you. You've given me a lot to think about.

"So, when is he coming?" Rose asked.

"Whenever he can rearrange his schedule. I'm sure he'll have to find a fill-in for his classes, and I don't know if he has any speeches or other things like that to reschedule, so I have no idea. He said he'd call and let me know."

All the way back home, she went over what her parents had told her.

Chapter 22

Two weeks went by, and there was no word from Justin. The autumn colors were breathtaking to Jackie. She had not seen the fall in the North for years and realized how much she had missed it. She marveled at how easily one forgets about the little things when one is removed from them for long periods of time. Jesse, on the other hand, had never seen such glorious colors in the trees before. In Texas, most of the trees were live oaks that stayed green year-round and only lost their leaves as the new ones pushed the old ones off. Oh, yes, there were trees that did lose their leaves but not with the brilliant oranges, yellows, and deep glowing reds as in the North.

Then after picking a basket full of apples from the orchard and entering into the kitchen, Grandma Craig told her that Justin was coming and would arrive on Friday afternoon and was looking forward to seeing all of them. Jackie's stomach did a flip. Mixed emotions began to churn within, feelings of excitement about seeing the one she vowed to love forever and dread at having to face him. She hoped he was dreading his face-to-face meeting with her as well. She went to her bedroom and got on her knees to pray. She prayed so fervently from her heart, to do the right thing, to be fair, to have empathy, to be patient and listen to what he had to say. Her lips quivered, and a tear escaped from her eye and ran down her cheek.

The week seemed to fly by, and Friday afternoon soon arrived. Jackie had fretted about what to wear when he arrived. She laid a dress on her bed, stood back, and stared at it. Should she get dressed up as though she were going on a date? She grabbed it and hung it back in the closet, deciding she didn't want to look so formal. She finally decided on her everyday clothes of jeans, T-shirt, and tennis shoes. After all, she was a farmer now, so why not look the part? She was done with San Antonio's high-society life. This made her feel more determined, more sure of her new life, and she wanted to show Justin how well she fit into it, how she wasn't ready to give it up for anyone, not even him.

He knocked on the door promptly at four o'clock, and Don answered. Not surprisingly, Don went outside instead of inviting him in. Jackie began pacing and glanced every few minutes at the door.

"Sit down before you wear a hole in the rug, dear," Maude said.

"I can't help it. What are they doing out there?"

"I'm sure Don just wants to have a little talk with him first, man-to-man. You know, he's very concerned about the way you've been treated too. He probably wants to know what Justin's intentions are with you, with your future, and with Jesse. You're acting like a cat on a hot tin roof. Come here, dear."

Jackie crossed to her grandmother, knelt by her chair, and looked into her grandmother's eyes. Maude reached out to stroke her hair, "Now I want you to take a deep breath." Jackie didn't move. "Go on, breathe," demanded Maude. "Deep breaths." Maude breathed deeply along with Jackie. "That's it. Now again. Deep." And they both took another deep breath. "Now don't you feel better?"

Jackie had to admit she did feel calmer. Then as she was rising, Don and Justin walked in the door. "Come on, Mom," said Don. "Let's take the car down to Mac's place. I need to talk to him about some things."

After the door shut behind them, it seemed so quiet. She wasn't sure if she was hearing the ticktock of the clock or if it was her heart pounding in her chest. She and Justin just stood staring at each other for what seemed like an eternity.

Finally Justin came to her, took her hands, and got down on his knees in front of her. "What can I do to make you forgive me?" he pleaded. "I will do anything if you'll forgive me."

Jackie remembered what her grandmother had just told her and took another deep breath. She removed her hands from Justin's, crossed her arms, and said a little prayer for patience before speaking. She squared her shoulders and began. "I need to try to understand why you said nothing when you left. So help me understand what went wrong between us. I really need to know."

He rose from the floor and said, "OK. But I want you to understand that nothing I did has anything to do with me not loving you anymore. My love for you has never changed."

She bit back her words before they came spilling out of her mouth. She had wanted to say, "Well, you sure have a strange way of showing me how much you love me." Instead, she said, "OK, go on."

Justin swallowed. "I know you want to understand, and I want you to understand, but I won't be able to tell you everything. There are some things I won't be able to tell you, and I'm not certain I should tell you any of it. But I can't live my life without you. You are more important to me than anything else in the world."

"You're talking in riddles, Justin. Just tell me why."

Justin took a deep breath. "I know this is going to be hard for you to comprehend. Look, can I sit down?"

Jackie agreed, and Justin continued. "The US government came to me a year and a half ago and asked for my help with a national security problem, as they called it. I can't go into all of that, but I agreed to help in any way I could. So, do you remember all those speeches I said I was scheduled to give?"

Jackie nodded.

"Well, there were no speeches. The government asked me to join a group on campus—infiltrate it, pretty much spy on them, and report what I found out back to them. At first, it was just going to their meetings, listening to what they said, and reporting back to the government. No problem, right? It was easy. But then things changed. The group became violent, and I wanted out. But the government said they really needed my help, that I had been very helpful, and to pull me out would leave them high and dry. They begged me to stay in the group, at least a little longer. And believe me, when the government wants you to do something for them, they have a way of convincing you it's the right thing to do.

"Anyway, because it was becoming more and more dangerous, I felt I had to protect my family somehow, and the only way I could think of so you wouldn't be in danger was to let you believe I had found someone else. I knew you would go back to Illinois where you and Jesse would be safe."

Jackie said, "So you're telling me there never was another woman? That it was just a ruse to get me out of Texas? Justin, I'm not sure I believe any of that. If that's true, why didn't you just come and talk to me about what you were doing?"

"I didn't because I knew if you went to Illinois knowing what I was really doing, you'd worry yourself sick about what I had gotten myself into, and you'd worry about my safety. I also knew if you knew the truth, you'd never leave Texas, and I needed to know you and Jesse were safe. And I also knew if you came to Illinois mad as hell at me, you'd be fine, and you'd be safe." He smiled at her. "Am I right?"

"I don't know, Justin. Maybe. I'm just not able to comprehend that you were a real spy. This is all so James Bond. Not real."

"I understand how you feel. And I agree with you. Believe me, I wrestled with what to do for a very long time. I gave excuse after excuse to the government about why I couldn't help them. I wasn't a spy. I was just a professor teaching history in a university. I have a wife and child to think about. What if, what if, what if. But when your government calls, how can you turn them down? And like I said, they can be very persuasive when they need you, and they can make your life miserable if you don't help them."

Jackie asked, "So what kind of club, gang—whatever they are—did you spy on?"

Justin said, "I won't tell you their name. I had never heard of them before I infiltrated the group. But when they began becoming more and more dangerous, I began looking for a way out."

"Dangerous how? What were they about?"

"They're against the government. They want to turn the United States into a communist country. At first, they just held rallies with placards against the government and marched around the campus and Austin's state capitol. Then they began to plan attacks on government entities. I wanted out. So I had to get out of it and fast. That's when I called the man over me and told him I was done, no more. I called you to try to convince you to go home. I was scared."

"So before I say I totally believe what you're saying, and I'm not saying you're a liar, but this is just a lot to swallow, I have a request. This man you say is over you, is it possible that I could call him? You know, just to make sure I'm not … well, not being fed some made-up story just to get me back? I mean, you say you can't tell me the name of the group, but you could at least let me talk to the man over you."

Justin reached into his pocket and retrieved his cell phone. "Absolutely. I'll call him right now." Then while he was dialing his phone, he added, "I know it's hard for you to swallow, but you must know I'm not a liar. I would never tell you something like that if it weren't true."

"But you did tell me something that wasn't true when you said you found someone else to love," she said, glaring at him.

The phone rang. Justin said hello, explained why he was calling, handed the phone to Jackie, and said, "His name is Kurt."

Jackie took the phone and said, "Hello, Kurt. I'm Justin Jacob's wife. Can you please explain who you work for?"

Kurt answered, "I work for Homeland Security, and Justin has been working for us for the past, what, year and a half maybe. He's been released from his duties now."

Jackie continued, "And while he worked for you, did he work undercover with some radical group on the campus where he taught?"

"Absolutely. And he was an invaluable asset for us. We're sorry he wanted out. But I understand that his family needed him, so we had to let him go. Let him know that if he ever wants back in, we'll be happy to take him." She thanked him and hung up.

"Now do you believe me?" Justin asked.

"I guess so. Still, I need time to think about all of this. So you sent Jesse and me away so we would stay safe. Right?"

Just then, Don and Maude came in the front door and apologized for coming home so soon. Jackie told them it was all right and that she and Justin would move to the front porch.

Once outside, Jackie said, "Justin, I just don't know what to say. I don't know how to react. I've had such bad thoughts of you, your cruelty in the way you treated me when you left. I … I need to think. Please go for now. Let's talk again. How long will you be staying here?"

Justin looked down at his feet. "OK, take as much time as you like.

I've got a room in town. I'm not leaving till we have everything figured out. Until I know I've got you back in my life." He took a step toward her, but she stepped back.

"Not yet, Justin. Let me think."

With that, he turned and left, stating he would call her tomorrow.

Jackie could hardly sleep that night. Things kept swirling around in her head. Questions began to surface. What should she do? She knew Jesse wanted her and Justin to get back together. Still, she had been so hurt. Could she really forgive Justin? She could understand why Justin did what he did. But it still didn't seem right that he didn't confide in her about what was really going on in his life. Had she been so wrapped up in her own life that she didn't notice the stress he was under? If she went back to him, where would they live? She knew she didn't want to give up what she had gained in Illinois. She needed to talk to him further. She was certainly happy that Jesse had not been home when he came by. How much of what he had told her should she reveal to her?

True to his word, he called the next day, and they set a time when he could come out to talk further. When he arrived, Jackie led him into the barn, where they sat on bales of hay in the loft. Jackie said, "First, I have to ask you if you've told any of this to Jesse."

He assured her he had not.

She continued, "Good. This is something I believe she has a right to know, but I think we should talk with her together." He agreed. "And if we do get back together, we need to decide where we are going to live, because I'm not going back to San Antonio. I've got a new life here. I'm close to my family, and I'm living here with Grandma and Grandpa to help—" Justin interrupted. "I don't care where we live. I've quit my teaching job, so I'm free. If you want to live here, that's fine. Just as long as I get my family back together."

Jackie looked shocked when he said he quit his job. She knew he really enjoyed teaching. "Why did you quit your job?"

"In order to get away from the group I had infiltrated. I doubt if they would have just let me walk away. I knew too many of their plans. I couldn't just say, 'Sorry, fellas. I quit. See ya.'"

"Wow! Helping the government really screwed you over, didn't it? You lost your family, and you lost your job over it."

"You're right about that. If I had it to do all over again, I would have told them to take a hike. I was happy doing what I was doing and didn't need them messing it up."

"You didn't let me finish what I was going to say about living with Grandma and Grandpa." Then she explained about the inheritance she would have if she agreed to live and take care of them until they died.

Justin seemed perplexed. "So you plan on being a farmer, a caregiver, mother, and hopefully a wife, all at the same time?"

"That's the plan."

"Does that mean we're getting back together?" He looked intently at her eyes, and she could clearly see the pleading in them.

"Justin, I never stopped loving you, even when I thought you were the worst person in the world. I just couldn't turn that off no matter how much I tried. And yes, you did a good job of sending me back to Illinois mad as hell at you. But I still loved you. And then I find out you and Jesse have been calling each other every Friday night. That was somewhat soothing to my soul, knowing you didn't abandon your daughter."

"So, should I go out and buy a pair of bib overalls if I'm going to be a farmer as well?"

Jackie chuckled at the mental picture. She couldn't wrap her head around that one. Still, if he was agreeing to live in Illinois on the farm, it would surely be nice to have a man around. Then a thought came to her. "Justin, I know how much you loved teaching, and I'd hate for you to give that up. What if you could teach at the U of I in Champaign-Urbana?" It's only around an hour away. You could still come home each night."

"Let's just take it one day at a time. I'll put that on the back burner for now. You never know. I just might like being farmer John, or rather farmer Justin." They both laughed. Then he continued, "I want us to sit down with Jesse tonight and have a long talk with her. Let me do the talking to explain how much I think she has a right to know and how much she doesn't need to know." She agreed, and then he said, "Can I hold you now?"

She fell into his arms and sobbed. She cried for all the hurt that had drained from her. She cried because she was so very happy. She cried because she knew Jesse would be happy. She cried because she couldn't believe how things were working out. Then she pulled away from Justin and said, "Just one more thing before we seal the deal. You've got to promise me *no more spy stuff* in your life! Agreed?"

They both laughed, and Justin replied, "Never again. I promise," as he wiped a tear from her cheek, cupped her head in his hand, and pulled her mouth to his. It was a long, passionate kiss, one that held no doubt of the love they had for each other.

The next day, Justin showed up at exactly ten, ready to do whatever they wanted. He was just happy to be able to spend time with his family again. Jesse was elated at seeing him, as he was of her. The three of them walked down by the pond and had their family chat with her.

Justin got the ladders loaded into the bed of the pickup and drove them over to the orchard with plenty of baskets for the apples. He set the ladders up in the trees, and they all began picking. When all the baskets were full but two, Jackie declared they should load them into the bed of the truck and use the last two baskets for the apples with bruises.

Jesse said, "Why don't we just leave them on the ground for the animals to eat? We don't need those apples. They're bad."

"We'll use them to make cider," said Jackie.

"But, Mom, they're rotten," protested Jesse.

"And that's the kind that make the best apple cider."

"Yuck! Is that what all apple cider is made from? Rotten apples?"

"Afraid so," Jackie replied. "At least the homemade kind."

Justin just stood there, arms folded, taking all this in. Finally he said, "You're really into this farmer stuff, aren't you, Jackie?"

"I love it. I never thought I would, but I really do."

"OK, Jesse," he continued as he bent down to pick up apples from the ground. "Then it looks like it's rotten-apple-picking time." He smiled at Jesse's smirk.

Soon they were headed back to the house. After the apples were unloaded into the cellar, they washed up for a glass of iced tea and lunch that Maude had prepared for them.

Afterward, Justin asked Jackie if she wanted to take a ride into town with her.

"No, not now. There's too much to do. There are apples that need to be put up for winter. Some we will leave in the baskets in the cellar, but we need to make some pies for the freezer, and there's jelly to be made and apple butter. And you and Jesse can take some apples to some of the neighbors while Grandma and I get started."

When Justin and Jesse returned, Maude and Jackie were up to their elbows in pie crust, and an apple pie baking in the oven filled the home with an inviting aroma. "Um, what's that wonderful smell?" Justin said as he entered the kitchen.

"Well, we couldn't freeze all the pies now, could we?" Jackie answered. "Will you be staying for supper, Justin?"

"Are you inviting me?"

"I guess I am."

"Then the answer is yes, I'd love to stay. Will we be having apple pie?"

Jackie couldn't help but smile. She knew he loved apple pie. "OK, now get out of my way and out of my kitchen so we can begin supper."

After the meal was over, Maude insisted on her and Jesse cleaning the table and told Jackie and Justin to get lost. They got into his rental car and drove to town, where he bought her a drink in the lounge of the only hotel.

"I've watched you all day, picking apples and working in the kitchen," began Justin. "I can see you are really happy here doing what you're doing. I think you'd really miss this if you came back to Texas."

"I really would," agreed Jackie. "I never thought I'd live to say I want to be a farmer, but I really do." Then she explained to Justin about the will her grandfather had drawn up, how she would inherit that home and acreage around the home, along with the pond, woods, and fields beyond.

He could see the sparkle in her eyes as she spoke, how excited she was. "I can see this is what you have your heart set on. So it looks like I've got some research to do about farming."

"All I know is this is where I belong. I feel it deep within. This is where I want to be—not just now but for the rest of my life. I'm home now, where I belong. And I think Jesse is really happy here too. She's made friends. She likes her school. And when she graduates, she wants to go to the U of I in Champaign. We have a life here now. A good life. There's no stress. No hurrying to one luncheon or committee meeting. No agenda to follow except my own. I love being here for Grandma and Grandpa in their old age. I love being close to my family, being able to see them often. I never realized how much I missed them until I came back."

Then she couldn't help but suck in her breath at her next words. It startled her to say, "Do you think you could be happy here with us?"

Never in her wildest dreams did she think he would be willing to move to a small town like this.

"I'd go anywhere as long as you were there," he answered. "I'm just not sure how good a farmer I'll be, but I'm willing to give it a try."

Jackie laughed. The thought of Justin out plowing a field was a picture she couldn't imagine. "You might end up hating me for making you leave where you are truly happy."

"I doubt that. I was getting bored with my job anyway. Maybe it was time for a change for me."

Just then, Ken and Stacy walked in. Stacy could not hide the shocked look on her face when she saw Justin with Jackie. Jackie waved them over to their table and introduced Ken to Justin. Stacy excused herself to go to the girls' room, and Jackie followed. As soon as they got there, Stacy was so excited she blurted out, "Why is he here? Are you two back together?" Needless to say, it took them longer than usual to return to their table.

When they returned, Justin and Ken were deep into conversation about construction, like they'd known each other for a long time. Jackie couldn't help but hope they would become close friends. It would be nice to have a foursome to do things with again.

Chapter 23

Next morning, Justin arrived at the Craig's home bright and early, ready for work. "I figured farmers get up at the crack of dawn to do chores, and I want to see just what they do at this ungodly hour. So, here I am, ready for work. What do you want me to do?"

Jackie smiled inwardly. "Have you eaten any breakfast?" When she found out he had only had juice and coffee, she insisted he sit and have a good breakfast before getting started.

Afterward, they donned their coats and headed out to the chicken house, with Jackie carrying her egg basket. As she called the chickens and tossed out their feed on the ground, Justin leaned against the hen house, just watching in wonder at the sight of his wife in a role he never thought he'd see. When Jackie looked up at him, she caught him smiling at her. "What?" she asked.

"Oh, nothing," he replied. "I just can't believe my wife has turned into a real farmer, jeans and all."

"Oh, stop!" she protested.

"You seem really happy at this. I'm glad."

"I am very happy. You would be, too, if you'd give it half a chance."

"Is that an invitation?"

"Well …" she said, letting it hang in the air. She turned, picked up her egg basket, and disappeared into the hen house, only to return a few minutes later with a basket full of eggs.

They walked back just in time to see a large truck roll up in front of the house. Jackie thought they had stopped for directions to a neighbor's home until Justin motioned for them to back into the driveway.

"What's this?" Jackie asked.

"You'll see," he said as he took out his phone and made a phone call.

The men unloaded quite a lot of treated lumber, shingles, nails, and other paraphernalia. They gave the men a cup of coffee after their job was finished and sent them on their way, only to have Ken arrive an hour later.

After he instructed Justin in what tools to gather up, the two men got busy in the back of the home, sawing, hammering, drilling, and making a lot of noise. By the middle of the afternoon, Jackie was delighted to see the form of a gazebo begin to take shape. She was delighted. When they took a break from their work, she let Justin know how pleasantly surprised she was. He replied, "I know you've always loved gazebos and have always wanted one, so now you're going to get one."

"Thank you so much, but you didn't have to do this."

"I know I didn't, but I want to. I'd give you the world if I could. You know that." Jackie looked down, not knowing what to say.

"Well, I'd better get back to my apple butter before Grandma has it all finished. As she walked slowly back into the house, she could feel Justin's eyes on her, watching her every move. When she reached the door, she turned to look at him. He gave her a wink.

After their evening meal, Justin asked Jackie if she'd like to take a drive. When he found a lonely road, he turned off the ignition and turned to her. "Do you feel like talking?" he asked.

"Justin, I want you to know that I understand how you were feeling. I do. Sadie and I had a talk, and she helped me to see that maybe we both became too wrapped up in our own separate lives to have any time for each other. And for that, I feel like I'm just as much to blame as you are. We didn't think about the needs of each other."

"I'm not blaming you for any of this."

"I know you're not. But I want you to know I'm sorry for neglecting you. I never meant to."

"I know that. And I never meant to neglect you. I don't think I decided to take on working for the government because I felt neglected. I just felt it was my duty. Believe me, you are not to blame."

"I'm glad that's behind us now. I want you to know though that I never want to go back to that way of life again. I never want to live in a big city again. I don't need that social life to be happy. I don't want the stress I know I was under then. I've come to love it here, the slower pace of life. And I love the country. It's so peaceful and quiet in the country. In the summer, when I'd sit on Grandma and Grandpa's front porch swing, I would close my eyes and just listen to the crickets, frogs, and an occasional nighthawk or owl. Sometimes, I'd hear coyotes off in the distance. It is truly relaxing. And I've learned so much about how to run the farm already. I know I have a lot more to learn, but that's been fun too. It's really a whole different world here. Sometimes, I have to pinch myself to see if I'm still alive because I feel like I've distanced myself from reality. I've come to learn the *real world* isn't just making lots of money or finding your place in the social structure of this world. The *real world* is living close to family, doing things to make others happy.

"Yes, I have to work to provide for myself, to put food on my table, but the work is so rewarding. I get so dirty in the garden, but when I look at the produce of my labors and how much I can share with others, it really lifts my spirits. I wish you could see how it feels, to experience this with me."

He smiled. "Oh I'm sure I will."

"Oh, Justin, I want you to, more than anything in the world. I do want to try putting all of this behind us and make a new life for ourselves here. I want you here on the farm working alongside me. And I pray you'll come to love the country as much as I do."

"Then may I take that as an invitation to move out of my room in town and move in here with you and Jesse?"

She smiled up at him and nodded. It was the only answer she could give because of the lump in her throat. She was so truly happy.

"Can I kiss you?" he asked as he put his arm around her shoulder as he leaned toward her.

"If you must."

"I must."

He pulled her close and held her tightly. It was a long, passionate kiss, full of all the love they felt for each other. Their breathing grew heavy. Justin began kissing her neck. Then Jackie said, "Justin, I think we should stop. There's too much work to be done, and besides, that's what nighttime is for."

He stepped back. "That's OK. I can wait. I can wait forever if I have to." Both were quiet for a while before Justin said, "I'll have to go back, pack everything up, and make my escape from everyone. Actually, it's better that I don't live in the same city as that unlawful group of kids on campus." He seemed to be talking to himself rather than to her.

"How long will it take you to do that?"

"Shouldn't take me too long. I don't have much since I gave you almost everything in the house when you left. I think I could get everything into a U-Haul that I could pull behind the truck." He jerked his head up. "That reminds me. You'll need a truck to work on the farm. Good thing I have one."

Jackie replied, "Well, Jesse ended up with a truck. But it's not a big one like you have, so I'm sure we'll use yours more than hers, and besides, if she goes to the U of I next year, I won't have the use of her truck much anyway.

"I want you to promise that we will never—and I mean *never*—speak of this again. I want to bury it forever. And I want you to promise to tell me if you feel like I'm neglecting you. We've got to have complete communication of our feelings and not keep them bottled inside us from now on. And I want us to never keep any secrets from each other again. If there's something going on in one of our lives, we have got to talk about it with the other one. Do you promise?"

"Definitely."

"Then let's go. I have something to show you." With that, she drove him to Ken's home to show him what he'd been working on for his bride-to-be.

Chapter 24

To Jackie, things seemed strained upon his return. He seemed to be constantly asking what he could do to help, what needed to be done, things such as that. In an effort to help with the adjustment, she began writing out a list each morning of chores he could do. Especially since he wasn't really skilled at carpentry, she wanted Ken to finish up the gazebo. It was coming along quite nicely, and she knew it would be her retreat in the backyard in the future.

Jackie heard there was going to be a hoedown at the Lawson's barn. Justin and Jackie weren't sure just what a hoedown was, but the Craigs explained it was a town get-together. There would be live music, dancing, good food, and plenty of liquor. The Craigs had stopped going a couple of years back because they didn't want to drive after dark, but they vowed that if Justin and Jackie would go, they'd be happy to ride along with them.

After eating and getting a few beers down, the band began to play. People filtered out onto the dance floor, and soon Justin turned to Jackie to see if she would dance with him. It had been such a long time since they had danced. Jackie tried but couldn't remember when it was. Soon she was being twirled around the dance floor in the arms of her beloved. She had almost forgotten how good a dancer he was, keeping time to the music flawlessly. Soon everyone was making room for them on the floor, stopping their own dancing to watch Justin and Jackie. Jackie was embarrassed and couldn't wait to retire to their table. After the song finished, Jackie headed back toward their table, but Justin caught her arm and pulled her back onto the dance floor as the band began to play a slow waltz.

Justin drew her close to him, and she laid her cheek upon his shoulder. He dropped his head down to the top of hers, and they gently swayed to the music. After a few minutes, Justin whispered in her ear, "You are the most beautiful woman here tonight, and I'm the luckiest man to have you in my arms. You feel so good. This is where you belong, and I'm so proud to be your man. I love the way your hair smells of perfume, and I love the dress you're wearing, how it shows your beautiful body. You are truly the love of my life, and I so want to spend the rest of my life with you. I promise you that we will never be apart again as long as I live."

Jackie looked deeply into his eyes and could see Justin meant what he said. She blinked back tears and managed a smile but couldn't talk because of the lump in her throat. She drew closer to him and laid her head back upon his shoulder, smiling inwardly that things were turning out the way they should be. She just hoped Justin would love living on the farm, working side by side for the rest of their lives.

Jesse watched her parents on the dance floor and began to relax. She knew they loved each other more than the world, and she hoped that someday she'd find someone who loved her as much as her parents loved each other. She felt she could concentrate on her studies now and make new friends and just have fun her senior year. She no longer had to worry about her mother being alone and trying to run a farm when she went away to college.

Jackie was happier than she had been in such a long time, and she smiled each time she saw Sadie in Ken's arms on the dance floor. The four of them talked and laughed when they weren't dancing. She also noticed how her grandpa couldn't help but tap his foot in beat to the music, even though they no longer could dance. They had many friends they could sit and talk with, and she knew they were truly happy to be able to come as well. This would truly be a night to remember. And Jackie mused that perhaps they just might have a hoedown in their barn someday.

As they were sitting and talking, Ken asked about Justin's plans for his future. Would he work outside the home? He let Justin know that if he wanted a job, Ken could use another hand on his construction crew. Justin thanked him for the offer but let Ken know that for now he planned on just working on the farm. After all, he didn't have to pay an exorbitant mortgage payment anymore. But he let Ken know he'd keep it in mind for the future if he came to realize he just wasn't cut out to be a farmer. They both laughed at that.

And Justin also said that if finances got tight with him not working, he could always sell a vehicle and use the old car Mr. Craig owned, although he couldn't imagine Jackie being happy with that. On second thought, he mused, maybe she would. She had certainly changed a lot since they had broken up. He could see her now as an entirely different person from the one he had known in Texas. He looked across the table at Sadie and Jackie deep in conversation and couldn't help but admire the woman she had become. Or perhaps she had always been the woman she was now, and he just never took the time to look at her closely enough. Jackie looked over at him then, and he winked at her.

Although he still had to admit, the part of Jackie that was always wanting to help those around her never had changed, and he couldn't help but smile when he thought about that because he was always so proud of her for her generosity.

He brought home a bottle of champagne one evening to surprise Jackie. He said they all needed a little celebration, for no special reason, just to celebrate life. They even allowed Jesse to have a little, but the Craigs declined, saying they didn't drink. Maude relented for just a little sip. They laughed at that. Jesse's expression after tasting it brought a round of laughter as she licked her lips and declared she wanted more. And Maude declared it burned all the way down, which made everyone laugh again. Justin and Jackie excused themselves from the table and headed for the front porch with the bottle and glasses in hand.

Jesse called out as they reached the door, "Don't bother cleaning the table up. I want to do it tonight." Justin and Jackie stopped and stared at each other.

"I wonder what's gotten into her," Jackie said. "That's not like her."

"Don't complain. Come on. Let's get out of here before she changes her mind," Justin said as he held the door for Jackie.

Fall was such a beautiful time of year, and even though it was already growing dark as they settled in the swing, the vibrant colors of the trees beckoned one last look before the sun set. Justin commented on them after they poured another glass for each of them. "I'm just blown away by the beauty of the fall here. I remember how we used to drive out around the countryside in Texas to see the fall colors, but the colors down there don't hold a candle to these trees."

"I agree," Jackie commented. She pondered this as she stared at the trees, sorry to see that they wouldn't last much longer. Before long, the leaves would be on the ground. She seemed lost in thought, and Justin noticed it.

"Are you all right? You seem like you're a million miles away."

"What? Oh, yes. Well, not quite a million miles but maybe a thousand. I was just thinking about what you said about driving out to the country in Texas. That seems like such a long time ago, and yet it seems like yesterday. And do you remember what else we would do?"

"Do you mean how we would find an abandoned road, park, and make love, or how we'd find a secluded spot on a lake and go skinny-dipping?"

Jackie smiled. "I knew you couldn't forget. We really did have some fun when we were young, didn't we?"

"We did," he agreed. "And we'll have more in the future. I promise."

They sat quietly sipping their drinks, listening to the cicada begin calling to one another and the frogs at the pond looking for a mate. Jackie couldn't help but think of how everything in creation had a mate, and it felt good to have hers back again. She felt warm and happy inside. Nothing needed to be said; they were just happy to be together. Justin eventually reached over and pulled Jackie close to him. She snuggled under his arm and smiled up at him as he lowered his lips to hers. It was a passionate kiss, one that would go into Jackie's memory as one of the best she'd ever had. She could feel the love and lust he had for her. She knew they wouldn't stay long on the porch.

Chapter 25

It wasn't long before most of the leaves were on the ground, and Jackie declared on a Saturday that Justin and Jesse had to help her rake them up. She wanted to burn them on the garden spot in order to turn the ashes under to amend the soil for her garden in the spring. They would rake the backyard into the garden spot, but she declared she didn't want the front yard oak leaves in the garden soil since they were too acidic. Justin smiled and said, "I'm so impressed with all you've come to learn about this farming stuff. You just never cease to amaze me."

"Well, I don't pretend to know it all, but," she said, winking at her grandpa, "I'm learning from the best."

"And you're a fast learner. I'll say that much," Mr. Craig said. "And, Justin, I've been meaning to ask you if you could put up a wire fence around the garden. We took it down when we gave up raising vegetables, but we've got lots of deer around here with the woods, as well as rabbits, and once they find out there's a garden, they can pretty much decimate it overnight. No hurry though, but sometime before the snow flies, so we can dig the post holes."

Justin agreed, but he'd never put in a fence before and wasn't sure just how successful he'd be at it. Jackie could read his facial expression and knew what he was thinking, so she said, "Don't worry. Mac can help you with it."

After putting on another layer of clothing, since there was a nip in the air, the three of them headed out to the toolshed for rakes and the leaf blower. Jackie and Jesse busied themselves with rakes, while Justin used the blower. Soon they had a huge pile in the garden plot, and before they could light a match to burn then, Jesse dove into the middle and buried herself. Justin laughed and joined her. Jackie told them to stay put till she got back, and then she ducked inside for her cell phone. Soon she was taking pictures of their faces poking out of the pile, their bodies completely hidden. Or at least Jesse's was. Justin was too tall to get his feet in. Then Jackie got a couple of good shots of the leaves filtering down around them while they threw them into the air. They rotated this way and that as they floated gently back to earth. Jackie did a slow-motion video of that, and they all agreed that was the best. Jesse traded places with Jackie, and she took pictures of Justin and Jackie. They ended the photoshoot with the two of them lying on top of the leaves, embracing each other, and staring into each other's eyes—eyes full of love. Jesse was so happy to capture it and vowed to develop the picture, frame it, and hang it on the wall in the house.

They brushed the leaves off, picked the remaining ones out of their hair, and lit the fire. Soon there was smoke billowing up, giving the yard an eerie look. Jackie again grabbed her camera and snapped some pictures of Justin and Jesse through the smoke, since they looked more like shadows than actual people. These were great memories they were making, and Jackie was so happy to have this time with her husband and daughter together, since she knew this time next year Jesse would be off to college, and this might be the last time they would ever play in the leaves together.

Justin came over to Jackie and put his arm around her waist, as if he knew what she was thinking when Jesse headed for the house for hot apple cider for them all. "She's growing up, Jackie," he said. "We can't stop that."

"I know." She sighed. "I wish we could keep her here with us forever, but that's being selfish, isn't it."

"You wouldn't want that for her, I know. I've seen young ones whose parents cripple them for life by trying to hold on to them. We'll have to let her go."

Tears stung Jackie's eyes. "I know, but I don't want to. She is so beautiful and good."

"Just like her mother," he said. "And I feel confident we've done a great job in raising her to be a responsible, well-adjusted adult. I'm sure she'll do just fine once she's out on her own. I said, 'We've done a great job,' but in reality, you're the one who's done it, not me so much. And you did a superb job."

"That's not true, Justin. I've always been so very proud of the way you took your responsibility as a father so seriously. I am happy that you were always there for her. You played with her when she was small and went to her ball games and other school functions. You never let your work interfere with your obligations to her. She always came before work, and I'm proud of you for that."

"You are?" he teased. "Then at least I'm not entirely rotten to the core."

"Oh, stop!" she replied as she punched his arm. "No one said you are rotten to the core. Maybe only half-rotten." She took off running, and he scampered after her. She dodged behind the large pine tree to escape his clutches and tried to duck around him to race across the yard, just as he grabbed her and pulled her close to him. His hands cupped her face as he peered into her eyes. Then he kissed her very tenderly, just as Jesse came out the back door.

"OK, you two," she scolded. "Don't make me come over there and break it up."

She carried the tray of mugs filled with hot apple cider and a cinnamon stick in each one to the picnic table and sat down.

Justin reached for a mug and said, "Your mom and I were just talking about how proud we are of the way you are growing up. We feel certain you will do well after you're out on your own. And I haven't had any conversation with you lately about what you plan to do with your life. I assume college."

Jesse responded, "Yes, I'd like to go to the U of I, but I know that would be very expensive, so maybe I will settle for Richland College. And especially now that you're not working, Dad, I really do want to go there."

Justin smiled. "And have you decided on a plan of action after you get there? Classes? Majoring in …"

Jesse sighed. "That I haven't decided. I love computers, but I'm not sure that's the way I want to go. It seems like every other kid wants to do computer work."

Justin said, "That's right, and now kids are graduating college thinking they'll get this high-paying job, only to find out they can't get any job at all. Have you got a second choice in mind?"

"Well, I've been thinking. I never have been around older people before moving here, but now that I've been around Great-grandma and Grandpa, I've really enjoyed them. They have lots of stories to tell. Stories about their childhood, growing up, experiences they've had, things they've seen. And well ... I've just kind of thought it would be nice to work around elderly people. Maybe I should consider going into the medical field. Nursing or something like that. I don't know."

"Well, it's still early in the school year. You've got a little time to consider your options before making a decision. But come January, you'd better be narrowing down your goal so you can get things lined up for college next year. Nursing is one career I doubt you'd ever lose a job in. There's always a need for caregivers and especially now that older ones are living longer. Think about that one a little more. I like that you've come up with that idea."

Jackie was busy raking the outer edges of the fire back toward the middle to burn up the remainder of the leaves but made sure she was in earshot of the conversation. She was so happy to have Justin there to help steer Jesse in the right direction. He never pushed her or demanded his way but kept the line of communication open with her by questions that could help her figure things out for herself. And he was always quick to praise her whenever he could.

Chapter 26

The first snow of the year came in the evening of November 20. Jesse was ecstatic since it had rarely snowed in San Antonio during her lifetime. She had heard they had had snow before, and she'd watched the news when most of Texas had lost power this past winter with the freak ice and snow, but her real memories of snow were when they had gone skiing in Colorado a few times. She donned her sock hat and coat and went outside to enjoy it. The flakes were small and began with just a few dribbling down at first, and soon they seemed to explode in size and number. She stood out in the middle of the yard with her arms spread wide, her face toward the sky, and began turning in slow circles as the snow began to accumulate on her face and hat.

Just then, Justin drove up and stopped to enjoy the sight of his beautiful daughter. He quickly grabbed his phone out of his pocket and began snapping pictures.

"Dad," she called, "can you believe it? It's snowing! Don't you just love it. It is so beautiful and so quiet. Look at the flakes under the light on the pole. They're really big and beautiful, don't you think?"

He came to stand beside her, looking up at the light pole. The snow was getting heavier and almost seemed to glow in the light. "Yes, it is beautiful, and yes, it is quiet. So, you think you're going to like living in this weather?"

"Oh, how could you not? I think this is just about the most beautiful sight I've ever seen! I hope we get enough snow that I can make a snowman."

"Well, if it keeps this up for very long, I can guarantee you'll get enough for a snowman. But one rule. You can't make a snowman without me, you hear?"

"Got it," she agreed as she began tromping around to see if there was enough snow to show her footprints. Justin reached the porch just as a snowball hit him in the back of the head and slipped inside his coat collar on his bare neck.

He turned and said, "That's it. You've had it," as he took off after Jesse.

She was giggling and had another scoop of snow already in her hands. She quickly let it fly toward his face. He ducked just in time and quickly tackled her to the ground. He scooped up a handful of snow and threw it in her face.

"No fair!" she cried. "You're bigger and stronger than I am."

"Don't start a fight unless you're sure you can win then," he replied as he turned to go back to the porch. As he stepped on the porch, he was hit in the back of the head with another snowball.

He turned again and headed her way as she let out a scream and at the same time laughed. He again tackled her, and this time his footing slipped, and he went down with her. They rolled around in the snow together, seeming to be fighting but in reality playing. He was enjoying the snow as much as she was. He couldn't pass up an opportunity like this one to play with his little girl in the snow. They laughed and laughed until their cheeks were pink from the cold and breaths were coming out in puffs of white. Then as they got up to dust themselves off, they noticed Jackie standing on the porch with her cell in hand.

"Hey, did you get that?" asked Justin. "She had to be taken down a notch. Shot me in the head twice with a snowball." He continued to brush off his coat.

"Looked more like you were the one getting taken down a notch," Jackie chided. "Better come inside and get warmed up. Grandma's got hot cocoa ready for you both."

The snow kept coming down all during the evening, and didn't let up until nine o'clock, after which Jesse declared she was heading back outside. Justin and Jackie told her they would go with her. So they all bundled up and headed out to walk in the new snow.

At first, Jesse just stood on the porch taking in the scene. The yard was completely covered, and she couldn't even see the walk. The light on the lamppost in the yard shined down on the snow, and Jesse exclaimed, "Look! The snow has sparkles in it!"

Justin and Jesse couldn't help but laugh. This was the first time Jesse had ever seen undisturbed snow. Even though they had taken her skiing, the snow had always been walked on or skied on, not light and fluffy like this was. Justin declared the snow to be perfect for making a snowman and began making a ball to roll around to make the body. Soon they were making individual balls to stack up. After it was erected, Jesse took off her scarf and hat to put on the snowman, while Justin dug under the snow, looking for sticks for arms, and Jackie looked for acorns for eyes. Soon they were standing back, admiring their work.

"Not bad, I'd say, for amateurs," Jackie decided, and Justin and Jesse agreed.

After that, Jackie gave Jesse her hat, and they all took off walking down the middle of the road. "I'd say there must be about four inches," Justin said. "Not bad for the first snow of the year."

"How much snow do they usually get here in the winter?" asked Jesse.

"Some years, quite a bit and all at one time, and it might hang around most of the winter, but I've been told lately not so much. Maybe someone knows we like snow and will give us more of it this year."

Jackie said, "Well, I know we might like it, but Grandma and Grandpa don't. They were telling me how they have to stay in because they're fearful they might fall and break a hip or something. If I had to just sit around all winter waiting for the snow to disappear before heading out, I'd hate it too. That must be really hard on older people. I'd go crazy before spring."

Jesse agreed. "So, what did they do before we moved in? I mean, how did they get their groceries in and things like that?"

"Oh, I'm sure the family made sure they had what they needed. They wouldn't have to go without food. And their cellar was full of canned goods, and their freezer too, thankfully. But still, to be stuck in doors for maybe months … well, I'm just glad we're still young enough to enjoy it. When I get old, I'll probably be cutting cloth to make a quilt like grandma does." They all chuckled at that.

They walked until they found themselves at Mac's house. They knocked and asked if he needed anything. They offered to shovel his walk, but he refused, saying, "Now, if you do that, what am I going to do? Besides, I've already lost the job of shoveling out your grandparents' I suppose."

"Actually," Justin said, "if you'd still like to do that, I'd be most obliged. Jackie and I've got work tomorrow morning, and Jesse's got school. I'll gladly pay you for it."

"I'll be happy to do it. And you're not paying me. I already owe you what with all the meals you've been supplying me with. Tell your granddaddy I'll be by nine o'clock sharp."

"Thanks, Mac," Jackie said. "I'll have a slice of hot apple pie and coffee waiting for you after you're finished."

"Can't wait," he replied. "Now you be careful out there. Gets slick when it snows. They should have the road plowed out by morning, but drive carefully tomorrow."

They headed back to the Craig's house for some hot apple cider to warm up.

Chapter 27

The Following Fall

Justin walked in after work to find Maude and Jackie up to their elbows in pitting and canning cherries. Jackie stopped, washed her hands, and, after wiping them on her apron, asked Justin if he wanted a glass of iced tea. He insisted on fixing it himself and sat down at the table to chat with the two women while they continued with the cherries.

He couldn't help but contemplate how happy he was to be back where he belonged in the family. Jesse was so happy her parents were back together. Jackie couldn't help but notice it in her achievements at school. Justin had to admit he'd been skeptical at first about leaving his work in Texas to move to such a small town, but after seeing how everyone in town had accepted him as one of their own, and seeing how the neighbors admired him even for being a part of such a well-respected family, he began to relax. Now, after two years, it was much better than he dared to hope it could ever be.

"What?" Jackie asked when she looked up to see Justin smiling.

"Oh, nothing," he replied. "I was just wondering who the proud recipient of some of your cherries will be this year, because I know there's no way we're eating all those ourselves."

"Well, I'm sure you'll help me deliver some to the women's league when we're finished putting them up. They deliver them to needy people, and I want to help with a donation of course."

"Of course," he said as he winked and smiled. "I'm always ready to help when I'm needed."

It had become a routine to deliver something or another to neighbors, whether they were in need or not, or to a local charity of some sort or a fundraiser for the school. Jackie might not be helping out volunteering any more at different charities, but she was nonetheless helping in a different way with her home-grown vegetables or fruit. She had learned not to become the organizer, which she feared would cause her to become too involved, taking her away from Justin, like it had before. After all, she had plenty of work to do on the farm.

"OK, I've sat here long enough," he said. "What can I do to help?"

"Well," Jackie began, "I planned on having dinner ready by the time you finished your chores, but you can see that didn't happen. Would you mind very much putting the chicken over there on the grill? I have a salad made already in the refrigerator, and I can throw some potatoes in the microwave."

"Consider it done," he answered as he rose from the table.

After he left the room, Maude said, "He seems very happy these days. And so am I."

Jackie sighed deeply. "Yes, he is. I think we all are. I was so afraid he would never do well here on the farm. He's never known country living. But I think he's done remarkably well for a city boy, don't you?" She let out a little giggle.

"Indeed I do," Maude remarked. "Now if we could just teach him how to milk a cow, we might just succeed in making him a farmer yet." They both let out a hearty laugh at that. Thought Justin had tried; he just couldn't seem to get the hang of it.

"Don't hold your breath on that one," Jackie said. "But you know, I never thought I'd see him planting a garden, or mending a fence, or doing some of the other things that have to be done around here. And I love having a strong man who can do things I could never do. He really has been a Godsend in so many ways."

"I'm just so happy for you and for him but especially for Jesse. Kids never seem to heal from a broken family, even if the parents seem to be able to move on."

Jackie stopped to meditate on that. "Yes, Grandma, I think you're right. I'm truly glad we made the right decision to get over that horrible past. But I have to tell you, if he had said he didn't want to move here to live, I'd have made a different decision for sure. I knew I was where I belonged, and I knew if he would just try it, he'd come to love living here as much as I do. And that's just how it happened."

"Yes, thankfully. And your grandpa and I feel so blessed to have you both here with us. This means the world to us."

Jackie leaned over to give her grandmother a kiss on the cheek. "We feel blessed to have you both here with us too."

That evening after they finished eating, Justin said he had an announcement to make. Everyone looked expectantly at him as he continued, "I have been contacted by a company and asked to head up a new department in that company. It would mean a substantial raise."

"Oh, that's great." Jackie beamed, even though she was hurting inside to think he had decided to begin working in the corporate world again.

"Not so fast," he continued. "It would mean we would have to move to Seattle."

Jackie's face fell. *Oh no*, she thought. *This can't be happening. We've been so happy here. I just can't give this up. I just can't.* She felt like she couldn't breathe, that her life was being squeezed out of her.

Justin continued, "But I told them no. I would never leave the home we've made here for any amount of money."

"Oh, Justin!" Jackie cried as she flew out of her chair and wrapped her arms around his neck.

"You know I could never take you away from here," he assured her. "Besides, I've got to admit this is the best life we could ever have, and there's no way money will ever get in the way of our happiness again."

Soon it was January and time for Stacy and Ken's wedding, Stacy asked John, Jackie's father, to walk her down the aisle, and he gladly accepted. Jackie was her bridesmaid, and Justin was the best man. The entire family from Stoner came for the wedding. And even though it was a small wedding by the younger generation's standards, it suited Stacy and Ken just fine. After the wedding in the country church just down the road from the Craig's, they all went back to the Craig's home for a nice meal. Then, just before dark, Ken announced that he was taking Stacy to her new home. He drove around the countryside just to give her a look at the country she would now be living in, he said. Stacy, of course, believed they were headed to the little house Ken lived in and was surprised when he headed into the woods up a rock drive about a half mile before reaching the house. "What are we going back into the woods for?" she asked. He just looked at her and grinned. She continued, "Really, Ken, we don't have to park in the woods to have sex. We're married now. It's legal."

Eventually, they came to a very large clearing in the woods, and there stood the most beautiful home Stacy had ever seen. It was huge, made of logs, and topped with a metal roof. The front of the home sported a large wraparound porch. She stared at the home and back at Ken, then back at the house again. He couldn't help but grin from ear to ear at her reaction. "Well," he said, "you didn't think I would let you live in that tiny little house down the road, did you? I couldn't let you make all those changes to the house you had planned." Then he chuckled.

"Ken, I … I don't know what to say! Is this where we are going to live? Did you build this for us?"

"Not for us. For you. I knew you weren't looking forward to living in the little house, and I'd already started building this before I even met you. Figured someday I'd get married, and I didn't want to bring my new bride to that little dump. Besides, I could just imagine you in this home but never could picture you in that little home."

He parked the car by the front steps, then came around and opened the door for her. He helped her up the stairs, stopped, and said, "Now just a minute." Then he scooped her up into his arms and carried her over the threshold into the home. Once inside, there was a very loud "Surprise!" as the entire wedding party sang out.

Stacy was stunned. "So you all knew about this? And no one said a thing to me? Jackie!"

Jackie just stood there smiling. "How could we break our promise to Ken not to tell? He wanted it to be a wedding present to you."

Stacy continued, "But where are all your cars?"

Ken answered, "I told them to park in the back so you wouldn't see them. And that's why we drove around for a while, to give them time to get here before us."

The only thing Stacy could say was "You little devil! And here I was thinking how quickly and easily I'd be able to clean and keep up that little house. Not so sure about this one."

Ken said, "The house is completely furnished, thanks to Jackie, Justin, and Jesse. All new furniture. But if there's something you don't like, I mean, it can be changed. You can change anything you want. And you can work from home because I built my office on the back of the house."

"Seems you thought of everything. And why would I want to change anything? Jackie knows my taste, and this is exquisite." She stood looking all around the room, into the kitchen and dining room, before she said, "So, are you going to give me the grand tour or not?"

They left the room then while the others popped a cork, gathered glasses, and began pouring the drinks. When they came back into the living room, everyone was seated all around the roaring fire John had built in the grate. Eventually, everyone decided it was time to let the newlyweds have their privacy and rose to leave.

Stacy went to Jackie, wrapped her in a big bear hug, and said, "Thank you, Jackie, for everything. And especially for giving me Ken."

Jackie hugged her in return and chuckled. "Oh, I don't think I gave him to you. After he saw you, I don't think I would have stood a chance anyway."

The next day, Ken and Stacy left for a honeymoon but refused to tell anyone where they were headed.

Justin and Jackie lay awake talking that night. "You know," Justin began, "at first, I was so apprehensive about living on a farm, not teaching anymore. Now I never want to see a classroom again. Never thought it would turn out so great."

Jackie turned to face him, put her arm around his waist, and said, "I'm so glad you're happy here. I worried that you'd get bored staying home so much."

"Bored?" Justin declared. "How could I get bored when there's so much to do? Chickens to feed, eggs to gather, apples to pick, gardens to plant, weed, and reap, leaves to rake, snow to remove, fences to mend—"

Jackie broke in with "And don't forget cows to milk."

They broke out laughing hysterically. Jesse knocked on the door and asked what was so funny, and they broke out laughing again.